CHANCE ENCOUNTER
❧ BOOK FOUR ❧

A PRIDE & PREJUDICE RE-IMAGINING

NEY MITCH

DEDICATION & AUTHOR'S NOTE

Readers, you all are phenomenally brilliant! I thank you all, am very appreciative, and I hope this finale is enjoyable for you—for I know how hard finales are to enjoy at all.

Special thanks to my family, publisher, editors, cover artist and everyone who worked on this book. You have all quite saved my life.

And a special thanks to Helyn Roberts-Vickers, who was willing to see this to the very end.

Once more, we reach the beginning of the end…

Ney Mitch

CHAPTER 1

PURSUIT OF THE TRUTH

*T*wo hours had passed since Darcy and Colonel Fitzwilliam had left to overtake Mr. Wickham and my sister.

Too stunned to eat anything, Jane, Kitty, Georgiana and I sat in my room, each of us equally disturbed.

At that point, we had spoken of practically everything that had been spoken of, yet we had no choice but to be redundant. All words poured forth, and we wondered how we had arrived at this moment.

"Wickham run off with Lydia," Kitty said. "How foolish I had been."

"Why do you say that?" I asked.

Kitty bit her lip and then continued.

"I will only continue speaking if you all promise not to hate me."

We all looked at each other.

"Did you know something about this?" Jane asked.

"Yes," Kitty said, guiltily, "please don't hate me."

"We won't," I assured her. "Now tell us the truth."

"I had seen Lydia a few times since we have been here," she narrated. "Remember that you encouraged me to, Lizzy? Well, when I did, I noticed some partiality for Wickham on Lydia's side. But I never saw anything on Wickham's side at all. He merely spoke to her in ways that he spoke to every woman. You know how he is, Elizabeth and Georgiana? He is a rake. Therefore, naturally, I just saw this as another of his flirtations that indicated nothing serious on his side. There was nothing to give me cause for feeling alarm. Yet, Lydia did once tell me one day that she felt that she would have the name 'Lydia Wickham' by the end of it."

Expecting us all to immediately begin to berate her, she rushed out her next explanation. "Please believe that I didn't think she was being serious. Jane and Lizzy, you know how Lydia is. She says things like that, so I just mistook her manner for being nothing more than the common way." Then she almost began to start weeping. "Please, believe me, I didn't know it was all serious!"

Instantly, Georgiana went to Kitty and held her as Kitty wept into Georgiana's neck.

"I didn't mean to be wrong," she repeated. "I didn't mean to be wrong!"

"It is not your fault," Elena voiced before Jane and I could. "Kitty, you are not to blame. As an eloper, the only people who are accountable for the blunder are the ones who committed the action."

"Precisely," Georgiana added. "My actions and Elena's must, ultimately, rest on our own shoulders, and Lydia's must rest in its proper place. And as a woman who has met Lydia, I do not believe that she would have listened to anything else but her own desires. I believe that everything still would have ended where it had, especially with the likes of Mr. Wickham. He deceives everyone!"

"And thus, you are not to blame, no more than I," I added. "Mr. Darcy, Georgiana, or anyone who has been deceived by Wickham."

"What sort of man is he that he has this power?" Elena asked. "I barely met him, so I do not know."

"He is handsome," Georgiana observed, "but there are many men who are equally so. For some reason, he is like that of siren, and he calls to you. Also, there is something about his manner that puts you at ease. It's as if he is looking into your very soul and connecting to it."

"And thus, making you feel special, when you mean nothing to him," I concluded. "That is his power, sadly."

"Well," Elena said, "those are always the ones that draw us in. Why is it always the terrible ones who have such allure, and the good ones repel us so much?"

"Who knows?" Kitty said at last, calming down. "But I can only suppose that it is the more flawed sides of us that bears the most confidence. That is why our terrible sides still thrive: it's because that side of us is so extraordinarily strong."

"You should write that down," I suggested.

"I already have," she said. "It was in the last chapter that I completed. How ironic now."

We were roused by a knock on the door.

We all looked at each other.

"If Mr. Darcy and the Colonel had returned," I deduced, "then they would not have knocked without calling out to us, but nor would they have sent a servant to tell us they were here."

Standing up, I walked to my door and opened it.

"Ah," Mr. Bingley acknowledged, smiling at us. "It is nice to know that I contacted someone."

"Mr. Bingley," Jane said over my shoulder, standing up, "good morning, sir."

"Forgive me," he said, staring past me and at Jane. "I hope I did not intrude."

"Not at all," I said, moving aside. "Please come in and be seated."

Willing to agree, he removed his hat and entered.

"How very fortunate that I was able to find someone," he explained. "I came here to issue a personal invitation. We are dining at the Lanes. My sisters and Mr. Hurst were wondering if you were open to joining our party. I, um…" He looked white in the face now. "I know that Caroline's last personal encounter was trying for you all, to say the least, and provocatively upsetting, to say the most. But she has informed me that she feels heartily sorry for her past behavior, and she will endeavor to improve herself as time progresses."

Jane looked at me.

"I thank her for her efforts to do so," I assured him, "and I respect that she is acknowledging her past behavior. Unfortunately, we cannot leave the hotel this day, for we are waiting for Mr. Darcy and Colonel Fitzwilliam to return."

"Ah. Yes, I tried knocking on their doors first, to see if they were present, but they were not there. Where did they go while leaving you behind?"

We all looked at each other again and I felt a blush stain my cheeks.

Reading our expressions, Mr. Bingley looked away, embarrassed.

"And I can see that it is something that I am not allowed to know," he rushed out. "Well, I suppose that I ought to go."

"We do not wish for you to believe that Mr. Darcy has not taken you into his confidence," I informed him, "nor that he and the Colonel have left us. There is a crisis which took them away quickly and gave them no time to inform you of it."

"A crisis?" he asked. "Good god, what is the matter? It is not your mother or Miss Mary, is it?"

"No," Kitty assured him. "Everyone who is at Longbourn is well."

"At Longbourn? Then… Miss Lydia?"

We looked at each other, avoiding his gaze.

"I see that I have pried too much," he said, "and I should leave now before I make you detest the sight of me."

"Mr. Bingley, wait!" Jane cried, and this halted him. Her cheeks red, she looked at me. "I do believe that we can confide in him."

"Can we?" I asked, then I stood up and faced Mr. Bingley, utterly indifferent. After all, it was Jane that was clearly still in love with him, while I viewed him as the friend to the ONLY man that I completely trusted. "Mr. Bingley, are you trustworthy?"

He started, uncertain at this direct question.

"Yes," he said, "I believe that I am."

"Then, if we tell you something in confidence, can you swear to secrecy? And, also, do not let this situation affect your views on us. It is a delicate crisis."

"Miss Elizabeth, Miss Bennet, Miss Kitty, Miss Darcy and Miss Elena," he stated, sincere, "whatever is the matter, I promise that I will not utter it outside of this company. Any information you tell me will die inside of me."

Turning to Jane, I resigned myself.

"He has promised. Tell him what you wish."

Mr. Bingley turned to Jane, eager.

"Miss Bennet," he said, "whatever you have to tell me, I hold to my promise. Also, if it is anything amiss, I promise to offer my protection… in any way that I can."

"Thank you, Mr. Bingley, that is very kind of you."

"No matter what," he pressed, "I am here. And I always will be."

His second assurance of this was unnecessary and exposed him. For it displayed his eagerness to appeal to Jane in every way, and love makes a person look a little foolish sometimes. We knew that we were witnessing two people who were in love, so, Kitty, Georgiana, Elena, and I looked away.

"I know that you will," Jane said at last. "Please, do be seated."

Mr. Bingley eagerly accepted, sitting down while Jane walked to the window and looked out onto the lawn. After a few seconds, she turned around.

"Mr. Bingley, the reason your closest friend and the Colonel have left us here is because they had received a report that is accurate. Our sister, in the dead of night, eloped."

"Miss Lydia?" he gasped. "Good god, with who?"

"With Mr. Wickham."

Mr. Bingley slunk back in his chair, his eyes angry—for the first time.

"Mr. Wickham!"

"Yes."

"That libertine!" he cried. "First, he hurts Darcy and now this?"

"Mr. Wickham has done more harm than you know, Mr. Bingley," Georgiana informed him. "To make you more aware, this is actually typical of him."

"Typical? And to think, all that time that we knew him in Hertfordshire, and he was this much of a villain? It's enough to confound all." He looked at us, empathetic. "I am sorry for you, but Darcy is an accomplished equestrian. He will succeed and get Lydia back."

At last, he turned back to Jane, stood up, rushed to her, and almost touched her cheek. At the last minute, he remembered himself and he lowered his hand, thoroughly ashamed of his own lack of control.

"We thank you for your concern," I said, helping to remind him to maintain propriety. "Your kindness is very appreciated."

"Yes, well, I said that I would do so, and I will hold to my word now. I am very sorry for this, but I do really believe that Mr. Darcy and the Colonel will bring Lydia back. Especially since they have only a couple of hours in between the pursued. I am of the suspicion that you wish to be alone now, to console with yourselves, but you must understand my confusion on the matter. My instinct is to stay here and keep you company."

"We would feel horrible if we kept you from enjoying the excursions that you planned for the day," Jane said.

"Say none of that. Brighton will still be Brighton and what is not done one day can be done the next. I will leave if you do not wish for my company, but I will despise myself for going. This is a dilemma that I wrestle within myself, but I have every right to ask for guidance. Can someone tell me, what is the right course of action? What do I do now? And what would make you all happy?"

I looked to Jane, who clearly wanted someone else to solve this dilemma.

"You are the eldest," I said, "you have the right to decide for us all. I'll let you decide, without protest, this time."

Jane was confused, so she decided to reason with herself.

"First," she began, "yes, I do wish for us to be alone, but I believe, Mr. Bingley, that your company will make us all so much more comfortable. There is nothing more wonderful than a friend at this time. However, I do not wish for you to break your excursion with your family."

"And I say that they will be satisfied with me going with them tomorrow. I shall take your words as encouragement. I am writing a letter to my sisters to tell them where I am."

He asked me for a pen, paper, and ink, composed a quick letter and had a servant send it to Mrs. Hurst's room. Thus, he spent the entire day with us, and we ate in Jane's and my room, telling Georgiana and Elena stories about when he moved into Netherfield Park.

All the memories of that time came flooding back to me. Father was still alive, mother was still a nervous embarrassment, though she did love us, I thought Mr. Darcy hated me, and the Netherfield Ball was what we had finally arrived at.

When speaking of this, Mr. Bingley and Jane gave the chief narration while Kitty and I added a few things. Looking on the two of them, I saw how Jane did still love Mr. Bingley, despite her affection for Colonel Fitzwilliam. If the Colonel had not pressed his own affection, then Jane would have accepted Mr. Bingley long ago.

"I see the Colonel!" Kitty cried, for she was seated by the window and had the best view of those who were coming and going.

"You do?" I cried, rushing up to her. "And Mr. Darcy."

Both men had returned…with no Lydia.

CHAPTER 2

THE MEN OF THE HOUR

*R*ushing out of the hotel, we met Mr. Darcy and the Colonel as their horses were being taken away.

"Elizabeth," Mr. Darcy cried when seeing me.

"I hate it when you go away," I exclaimed, rushing toward him. Taking me in his arms, we forgot ourselves and kissed each other passionately right in the front of the hotel.

Eventually, we separated to see the rest of our party standing there. Mostly they were huddled around Colonel Fitzwilliam, preparing for news, but Mr. Bingley naturally stood on the outside of our company.

"We told Mr. Bingley," I whispered to Darcy. "He promised that we could confide in him."

"I'll make sure that he does," he assured me.

Unashamed, we joined the rest of our company.

"You come without Miss Lydia," Georgiana noted. "Does that mean..."

"It's best to discuss this within," Mr. Darcy advised. "Come. We'll talk of this in my quarters."

Following his instructions, we went upstairs again, went to his room, and he ordered coffee and refreshments brought to us at once. As well as some cold meats, bread, cheese, and stew.

"That is good," Kitty said. "We haven't really eaten all day."

"You haven't?" Colonel Fitzwilliam asked.

"We were too worried to eat," Jane explained. "We had tea, but other than that, we had no appetite."

"For once, I understand what Mama says when she says that she is stricken by her nerves," Kitty said. "Mind you, she could still eat. Oh, imagine if she had ever learned of this!"

"Well," Mr. Darcy said, "you all shall have an appetite now. We found them."

We all suddenly became animated.

"You did?" I cried, very much relieved.

"Oh, thank god," Kitty professed.

"When we saw that you came alone…" Jane trailed off.

"You don't see them with us," Colonel Fitzwilliam explained, "because upon retrieving them, we transported them back to Old Ship Hotel, where Colonel Forster has detained Mr. Wickham, and Mrs. Forster is watching Lydia. And probably giving her a good lecture."

"We assumed that *that* would be the best course of action, as opposed to bringing them here," Mr. Darcy said. "For if we brought them to the Grand Brighton, scenes might arise that were unpleasant to everyone. I do not mean to disrespect Miss Lydia, however…"

"She might cause a scene," Jane finished his sentence.

"Not might," I confirmed, "but she *would* cause a scene. For one reason or another. But now that I think about it, when you found Mr. Wickham, how was he when you overtook them?"

"Typical Wickham! He offered lies about their running off together, but when we separated them both, Wickham eventually gave way and confessed that he was leaving Brighton because of debts he had incurred."

"Then what did Lydia have to do with it all?" Elena asked. "Stealing away with her would hardly seem like the best course of action, for it is evident that she was not friendless."

"A man like Wickham is wanton," Colonel Fitzwilliam explained, "and sometimes cannot see past the immediate relief of his desires. He wished for Lydia to come along with him, because she wished to, and because it would have satisfied his desires."

"Yes," I said, "it was not in his best interest, other than that... and the other matter of his wanting revenge."

Everyone turned to me, astonished.

"Lizzy?" Kitty asked. "Whatever are you talking about?"

"Mr. Wickham has entertained an idea that I have slighted him in some way," I elaborated, "and therefore, he holds me in contempt now. And we all know that Lydia liked him immensely. The idea of running off with Lydia would naturally satisfy any feelings of resentment he had toward me and serve as recompense for his imagined slights. Mark my words, there was something personal in all this."

"How monstrous," Elena commented.

"How Wickham," I confirmed, playing on her words.

The food came and we all sat down to eat eagerly.

As we did so, and the servants left, Darcy turned to Bingley.

"I was told that you were made acquainted with our situation," he began.

"I was."

"Mr. Bingley came upon us soon after you left," Georgiana explained, "and he remained with us the entire day."

"That is what I would have expected of you," Mr. Darcy replied, looking at his friend. "Offering comfort to our left-behind company. You have made me proud, Bingley."

"The pleasure was all mine," Mr. Bingley responded, "though I regret the reason for your mission, it placed me in the position of being around such friends. Therefore, even in the eye of the tragedy, I found joy."

"We owe you much for supplying the camaraderie that they needed at present," Colonel Fitzwilliam also added, offering friendship between Bingley and himself.

"Of course, though my heroics are meagre compared to yours."

"And that is the main part of it," I said. "Who knew that we would have such heroes in our midst. Really, gentlemen, you have deceived us so very much. We knew you to be good men, but not this gallant."

Mr. Darcy's eyes twinkled.

"I don't know if I should be upset that you had so little faith in me, or happy for you complimenting us."

"I order you to take the compliment and leave out all the rest."

"Very well. In this moment, I will obey."

"And to think," Jane augmented, "that this morning, we were in such a state of agony, and now all is put to rights. A change of fortune, so great in so little time, is so wonderful."

"I agree," Kitty said. "Imagine if the worst had happened. Imagine if Lydia and Wickham did successfully run off together, and, since Mr. Darcy has confirmed that Wickham was never inclined to marry Lydia, she would have been lost for quite some time before she was found again. It would have been an elopement that would have gone on for months."

"If that would have happened," I pointed out, "then Mama, Mary, and the Gardiners would have discovered this. And potentially, the rest of Hertfordshire might have heard about it. If that were to occur, I believe that would have driven Mama into hysterics and that would have broken her nerves into more pieces than they are already. Mr. Darcy, Colonel Fitzwilliam, and Mr. Bingley, I have a request to make."

"What is that?" Mr. Bingley asked.

"Don't ever change. If you were to do so, that would be a very indelicate business."

"A request for things to stay the same," Colonel Fitzwilliam said with a grin. "Yes, I think I could succumb to that demand."

"I must say, Elizabeth," Mr. Darcy responded, "your demands are very logical today."

"My demands are logical every day. I may not always be rational, but I am always right," I joked. "Well, except for all the other times that I clearly have not been right. Yet let's not count those."

After the dinner ended, we parted ways and Jane did her customary habit of looking for a spider in our room so that I could have a moment alone with Mr. Darcy.

"Moments of intimacy in a hall," I noted. "This is what our lives have come to."

"You kissed me in the street," he observed. "That gives me the right to kiss you whenever I want."

"I will kiss you if you grant me one wish."

"You make a lot of demands."

"I want us to be one in all things."

"Very well. What is this wish?"

"I know that you are going to see Wickham again. Might I ask permission to go and see him with you?"

His face changed.

"Lizzy…"

"I do not want you to be upset over this, but I have to see him."

"Why?"

"I promise you, there is no reason to get jealous. I am doing this because I have a plan."

"What plan?"

"This might be the only way to wake Lydia up and make her see her true self."

"How so?"

"I'll tell you tomorrow when we go. I would tell you now, but we have very little time before Jane comes to retrieve me. I don't wish to spend the remainder of our time talking when I owe you a kiss."

He brightened up.

"I tire of waiting."

Quickly, he pulled me to him, and our lips pressed against each other's before I even knew it was occurring. The suddenness of it was most invigorating, and I was lost in the beauty of the moment.

Caring not for how we would look in the eyes of any passers-by, I fell into his embrace, knowing that he loved me, despite that we were still not wed.

After a minute of this, we heard the door open, and Jane emerged.

"No more spiders, Elizabeth," we heard her say. "All is well, and no tragedies are on the rise."

At last, my lips parted from Mr. Darcy's, but we continued in an embrace and our foreheads resting against each other.

"This morning, I woke up in despair," I whispered, "and I go to bed knowing that the crisis has been averted. You saved us."

"You saved me first."

"I love you."

"And I love you."

At last, we parted, and I disappeared into our room.

As we got into our nightgowns, I turned to Jane.

"I know that our displays of public affection are not proper," I began, "but we cannot help it."

"I understand why you do as you do," she said, removing her stockings. "It is just that... I realized something."

"What?"

"I never saw our parents kiss. Did you?"

Sitting up, I thought about it.

"No," I realized, "come to think of it, I never did see them kiss each other."

"And of course, I never saw any of our aunts and uncles do that either."

"Nor have I."

"Me as well. When I first saw a man and woman kiss were tenants on our estate, and when I asked Mama what they were doing, she did not explain it very well. I suppose that she was too embarrassed to. Hill had to tell me what it all meant."

"How extraordinary."

"And then you kissed Mr. Darcy and he kissed you, in public, and there was no cataclysm that occurred, no uproar, no controversy, or thunder striking the heavens. It was all done so innocently."

"Yes. It makes one wonder who was the first imbecile to teach the habit of spouses not being able to show affection for each other in public. Whoever they are, they have much to answer for."

"That is what I want," she said at last.

"What do you mean?"

"I want that sort of love," she said. "I want the love that you and Mr. Darcy have for each other."

I stopped brushing my hair and looked at her, surprised.

"Really?" I questioned.

"Yes."

"Jane, I never would have thought such."

"I know that I do present a different image than how I feel. But I want—passion. I want a man to feel it deeply for me."

"I believe that Mr. Bingley and the Colonel do feel that way."

"You think so?"

"Yes. They are just not allowed to show it. Remember how Mr. Darcy and I first met. He was stiffer than marble. He would not budge or show any romantic inclinations, because he was laboring under the weight of propriety. Once that weight was removed from him, he displayed a more open side. If and when you make your choice, perhaps it will be the same."

"Or perhaps it won't. Perhaps their love will stay restrained."

"If you worry about it being so, then you can always tell them this, so that they will try to change their behavior."

"I could not do that!" She gasped.

"Yes, you could. Jane, the only way to be happy in life is if you speak up sometimes. You cannot blame a man who loves you for not meeting your expectations, if you never told him what those expectations are."

I got into bed and opened a book.

"Think about my advice before you fully dismiss it."

"I just feel like I would be too scared to do it," she admitted.

"I understand why. Confrontation is an intimidating thing. Sometimes, it is easier just to let things remain as they are. But if we all did that, then nothing would ever change, now would it?"

She got into her bed and looked up at the ceiling.

"There is no right or wrong answer to this dilemma, is there?" she asked.

"No, there is not. That's what makes it all the more fascinating."

Eventually, we snuffed out the candle and watched the darkness.

"This morning, I thought tragedy had struck us again," she voiced.

"Me too."

"And for us to have escaped this all, is so fortunate. But it's not simply fortune. We had something on our side that we didn't have before."

"What?"

"Friends. We had real friends."

"Yes, I suppose that we did."

Soon, we both fell asleep.

The next morning, Colonel Fitzwilliam came to us after breakfast, to take us to see Mr. Wickham. Before we set out to depart, Elena came to us.

"Colonel," she appealed to him, "I know that I should ask for nothing more, but I must ask."

"Yes, Miss Elena?"

"Can I go with you all, so that I can speak to Mr. Martin again? It is just that… well, he is the reason that we were able to learn of Miss Lydia's plight. It seems only right that I thank him for trying to achieve his penance."

Colonel Fitzwilliam considered this very quickly.

"Very well," he said, "I suppose that he has redeemed himself, somewhat."

"We should see Mr. Martin first," I suggested, "so that you can leave us after your interview with him, Miss Elena. I don't wish for you to linger when I am speaking with Mr. Wickham. It might be a long discussion and you shouldn't have to wait for us."

Miss Elena said, "I am content with that."

The four of us set out to Colonel Forster's headquarters, and we met him eagerly. When we told him our plans, he was not surprised.

"So, you first wish to see Mr. Martin and then Mr. Wickham?

Naturally. But I must say, in all my years, I have never had a more unsatisfactory time with officers in so short a time. Thank goodness Mr. Martin belongs to you, Colonel Fitzwilliam. If he belonged to me, the stress would force me to retire to Bedlam."

Granted entry, we sat in the detention area and at first, Mr. Martin was brought to us.

Mr. Darcy, Colonel Fitzwilliam, and I sat in a corner as far away as we could, to give them a sense of privacy. In truth, we could hear everything they said.

When Mr. Martin was brought in, he sat opposite Elena, and they faced each other.

"I heard that you were flogged," Elena began. "I hope that you have healed."

"I have," Mr. Martin responded. "Yes, thank you. I acknowledge that it was a just punishment, and I did deserve it."

"Yes," she responded. "Forgive me, but I am a spiteful woman. Despite that you have helped us, I suppose that there is a part of me that will always want revenge. In truth, I am not sorry that I am this way. I like believing that people should suffer for their offences against each other. Because if we did not, then what is the point of trying to be good if the evil still thrives and never gets corrected? Not that I am calling you evil."

"But I was."

"I thank you for admitting that you hurt me."

"I couldn't stand being poor anymore."

"I understand the fear of poverty, but I shouldn't have had to pay the price of your pain." Wiping the air, she dismissed the topic. "But we should say no more of that. I came to thank you. By deciding to help us, you might have saved the life of another woman who did not deserve what the man intended for her. By choosing to help, you did a lot. In this moment, Mr. Martin, you are a hero."

"If you are to thank me, thank me only for yourself. It was you that I thought of when I chose to reveal Wickham's schemes. We all have the right to be forgiven if we apologize in the right way and try to correct our mistakes. I cannot take back what I did to you, but I see that you have the family that you always wanted now—

the family that you told me that you never had before. If you were to be happy with them, then they didn't deserve the same scandal that I put you through. But you do forgive me."

"Yes, I do. I admit that I do not know if I will ever look at you as being more than an acquaintance. But for the moment, I am happy that you chose to be a good man."

He raked his fingers through his hair. "Thank you. That is a burden that is lifted from my shoulders. I just did not think I could suffer from day to day, knowing that you could not stand the memory of me."

"The past still hurts me, but this present will be my lasting memory of you. You have your goodness now, Joseph. Keep it."

Their interview ended soon, and Mr. Martin was taken away.

Finished, Elena turned to us.

"How do you feel?" I asked.

"Alive," she answered, "very much alive."

Colonel Fitzwilliam escorted Elena back to the Grand Brighton and Colonel Forster sat with us as we waited for Mr. Wickham to be brought in.

Eventually, Mr. Wickham entered, guarded by two soldiers. Colonel Forster dismissed them as soon as Wickham sat down.

Wickham's expression was difficult to read. Seeming to have decided to appear complaisant, his face was calm. But still waters have been known to run deep.

That being said, his expression marked a contrast between himself and Mr. Martin. The latter had looked humbled, while the former looked as if he was preparing himself for a painful scene to arise.

I sat at the desk and Mr. Darcy sat in the corner. Immediately, I felt Mr. Darcy's body shift and grow more defensive.

"Miss Elizabeth," Mr. Wickham began, "you look remarkably well this morning."

"Are you serious?" I asked, completely unwilling to succumb to the typical way a person was supposed to respond. Rather, I preferred to get to the heart of the matter. "Mr. Wickham, I understand that flattery is your main weapon, but you cannot believe that it is going to improve anything."

His face grew resigned, and for a second, I saw seething rage come across his face before it was masked by indifference again.

"Ah," I augmented, "there it was. The true look of Mr. George Wickham. It danced across your face for a few seconds and then you hid it under your many masks. I'm not afraid of your true self, Wickham, not anymore. Could you do me the favor of showing me that true side again? That is the side of you that I want to talk to. It may be vicious to behold at first, because I am not used to it, but that seems to be the side of you that has any truth to it. Wickham, please, let me see that side of you again. Because that is the side of you whose help I need."

Mr. Wickham leaned back in his chair, looked away from me and at the wall opposite us both. Finally, he looked back at me, and his eyes contained the wrath again.

"Ah," I responded, and for a second, that was all that I could get out. His true self really was frightening to behold. Perhaps if I was used to it, it wouldn't have startled me so much, but since this anger was etched across a face that spent his entire life presenting another mask, the change was extreme. Next, I collected myself, and my courage rose again to its traditional place. "Mr. Wickham, as he truly is."

"You asked," he responded. "I've always had a hard time denying you anything, though you always found it easy to deny me such."

"That is not true, and you know it," I argued.

"It's not?"

"I once believed you," I confessed. "I once believed everything you told me and defended you against anyone who slighted you. And you made me into a fool."

Mr. Wickham looked past me and at Mr. Darcy.

"You won," he said to Darcy. "You always win."

"That had better not be what this was all about," Mr. Darcy responded. I looked between both men and felt as if I had stumbled upon something that went deeper than myself.

"Colonel Forster?" I asked.

"Yes, ma'am," Colonel Forster responded.

"Can you leave Mr. Wickham in shackles, then leave us alone? I think it would be better for all."

"Yes," Mr. Darcy stated with finality. "Miss Bennet knows my desire to not have my private business exposed for little reason."

"Understandable, sir," Colonel Forster said, ordering one of his officers to shackle Mr. Wickham's hands behind his back. After doing so, they left the room, and I was alone with the Pemberley men.

"Now," I asked, "what is the truth behind you both? And what devilry did you bring to Hertfordshire?" I asked Wickham.

"The devilry of a man who could never forgive me for being born more fortunate than him," Mr. Darcy answered, looking at his childhood friend. "For once in your life, just admit it, George. You were jealous of me."

"Of course, I admit it!" Mr. Wickham roared. "I may have been afraid to once, but now I know that's what it is and has always been. For god sakes, Darcy, you have your money, your position in society and Pemberley—but you had to have Elizabeth too. You couldn't help yourself."

"I loved her before you ever met her. And that was after you used Georgiana."

"I apologized for that."

"You apologized! You lied about what happened, ignored the villainy that you did there, and slandered me in the process."

"Not just Mr. Darcy either," I added, "but Wickham, you told me that Georgiana was proud, and you slighted her character."

"I was angry," he admitted, his tone gentler. "I was angry at her for taking her brother's side against me. I admit that she deserved better."

"She never deserted you," Darcy corrected. "I threatened that you would not receive her dowry if you married her, and you deserted her."

"I was delusional from my anger," Mr. Wickham said, "and I told myself that Georgiana agreed with that scheme of yours. Even if she did, I never should have been angry with her. I know that now."

"You know this now?" I asked. "After you ran off with my sister."

"Lydia wanted to run away with me, and I wanted company."

"You could have said no."

Wickham looked away from me and at the wall again. His eyes were looking into an invisible distance as he spoke again—to himself.

"Be a good boy, George. The world is your oasis, but we shall teach you to not look. Oh, but you can look, but you cannot touch. Oh, you can touch, but you cannot taste." He turned back to me. "People tell me that often. That is the lesson that rules our lives, isn't it? There is so much of life to offer, and yet we deprive ourselves of so much happiness. Don't you ever notice that? If a young woman wants to run off with me, that is her business. We should have the right to enjoy each other's company in the way we wish. Whose business is it if we do that? We don't hurt anyone, but the world acts as if you have committed murder. If you want to gamble, then you are a villain. If you are a gamester, then you have no right to enter society. If you flirt, then you are a rake. How much of life are we stealing from ourselves with these restrictions? I am a man who was born with every appetite that a man can have. Then the world tells me to quiet that part of myself, to ignore it, to act like it does not exist. No one can be half a man or half a woman. All we can be is ourselves. I tried to be the good man that the world tells me to be, and I was not good at it. So, I handed the living over and took those 3,000 pounds and lived life like the gentleman that I wished I was. And I ruined myself."

"So, you came back and wanted the living and more money," Darcy responded, "and you are about to justify yourself."

"I just don't know what I am," Wickham responded, "what I want, and how much I want. I just know that I want everything… and yes, I forgot that I had to work for it. Does that surprise you both? That I am not making excuses for myself anymore? I suppose I am tired. Usually, when a man feels as if he has lost it all, he expects the dread and agony to sink in, but that's not what is happening now. I'm just resigned."

I looked at Darcy, who also was at a loss. Faith, I think neither of us expected this reaction.

"Mr. Wickham," I began, "I am sorry for any pain I caused you, and I did wish to be your friend once. But I am not sorry for not trusting you, not relying on the veracity of anything you say, and for seeing your inability to see anything clearly." Leaning forward in my seat, I placed my hands on the desk. "Perhaps you were jealous that Mr. Darcy had everything that you didn't, but that excuses nothing. Rather than appreciate your lot in life, and use it to better yourself, you only raged against the people who were more fortunate than you, despite the fortune they had shared with you. And yes, life is a cage that society places on us, and we spend our lives trying to seek freedom in the best way we know now. But guess what? Everyone goes through that, so I would recommend that you get over it! You had a great life, Wickham. More than most. Therefore, that was not enough of a reason for you to turn around and hurt so many people. I am sorry for any pain you felt, but never sorry for remembering the pain that you gave to others. Others who deserved better."

Wickham was silenced by this, so I continued.

"And now it is time for you to admit that your plight with Lydia was not just something done to satisfy your carnal desires. I am sure that it is part of it, but not the whole thing. I know that you are not in love with Lydia. You never have been and never will be. But you did once propose to me, I refused you, and now you elope with my sister. The coincidence is not that hard to recognize. You have confessed that jealousy leads to you doing rash things, in the name of revenge. I am strong enough to hear it. Wickham, did you do this out of any motive to get your revenge against me?"

Wickham did not answer at first

"Wickham," Mr. Darcy said, "answer her."

"Yes," Wickham said at last. "Yes."

I closed my eyes, happy that he was finally able to admit it.

"Then you can help me," I concluded.

"What do you want from me?" he spat. "You have the truth, now let me go to prison for my debts and laugh at me from a distance."

"I am going to discharge your debts. I will pay all that you owe from the small legacy that I am left," I magnified.

Hearing this, Wickham turned to me.

"What?"

"I didn't stutter, Mr. Wickham."

"Why? Why would you do that?"

"In payment for what I need you to do. Lydia will never be easy and willing to return home peacefully unless she sees the truth. I need her to see the truth."

I told him my plan. When I finished, Wickham was silent.

"Well," I said, "will you help me? When you do so, I will discharge your debts, leaving me excessively poor, for the sake of my sister's soul. But also, by doing so, we are done, Mr. Wickham. You have a habit of seeking revenge on people, for reasons that they do not deserve. I need you to promise me that you will improve from this day forth. You need to overcome the darkness inside of you, and no longer punish others for your life. And if you don't, and we hear of other ladies being disturbed by you, of large debts being made, then we will have no choice but to intervene. Will you agree to this, Mr. Wickham?"

"I…"

"Yes?"

"You know your sister; she does not always listen."

"She will listen if you phrase it correctly."

"I see your point. Elizabeth?"

"Yes?"

"I am sorry."

"Are you?"

"Yes. For everything." He turned to Mr. Darcy. "With us, it's more difficult, isn't it?"

"I can never forgive you for all that you have done to me," Darcy admitted.

"And I can never forgive you for having the life that I wanted," Wickham admitted. "At least we are honest with each other." He turned back to me. "I will do everything that you ask. And as for the darkness that is within me, I do not know how long I can keep it quiet."

"If you manage self-control, then you will."

We had Colonel Forster send for Lydia and were not left waiting for long. Soon she arrived, and she looked excited when she saw Mr. Wickham.

"Darling!" she cried. Rushing up to him, kissing his head and running her fingers through his hair. "It has been an eternity since I have seen you. Mrs. Forster is upset with us and is angry at me for running away. You need to talk to her, because you will convince her that we are in love and that nothing else matters."

"Because family means so little to you," I announced. Finally, Lydia turned to Darcy and me.

"Lizzy, what did you and Mr. Darcy do!" she cried. "I should have known that you both would get in the way. Elizabeth, don't you understand that I was going to get married? You know our situation at home. It's only a matter of time before we lose Longbourn! We have no home. And here I was, about to succeed as our mother tells us to, and you both ruin the happiest moments of my life."

"If it was a correct arrangement," Darcy stated, "then why were you running away in the dead of night?"

"It was going to be a secret," Lydia argued. "Wickham arranged it perfectly, and we were going to surprise everyone."

"The only surprise would have been us discovering that you had ruined the family," I compiled, "because you ran off with a man who had no intention of marrying you."

"Elizabeth, how could you be so evil to say something so horrible to me?" Lydia cried. "I am never speaking to you again."

"What she said is not horrible, but accurate," Mr. Wickham

interjected, removing Lydia's hands from his hair, and moving away from her.

"Accurate?" Lydia laughed. "Wickham, what are you talking about?"

"I'm talking about the fact that I don't love you," Wickham acknowledged. "About the fact that I fled Brighton to escape my debts, and I just took you along for the ride because I wanted company—I'm hedonistic in that fashion, and I do not apologize. I had no intentions of marrying you, and I never will."

Lydia looked at him, then at me, and then she rolled her eyes.

"That is all not true," she protested. Then she gave me an evil eye. "This is all your fault, isn't it? And Mr. Darcy, everyone knows how much you abused my dear Wickham! Neither of you can be trusted."

Walking up to Wickham, she took his hand.

"I know how spiteful they can be. I know that they are clearly making you say these things because they are cruel. You don't have to give in because they have scared you. I am going to wait for you, and we will triumph over them all!"

"Stop it and shut your ugly mouth!" Wickham spat, pushing her hands off him. "No one is making me do anything. I mean what I say. I was never going to marry you. For how could I? I love an open woman, but there is a severe difference between an open woman and a ridiculous one. You are young, and that excuses so much, but how do I know that you won't grow up and still be like this? Men do not want stupid wives. And that's what you would be! Why would I enter an arrangement where both you and I would make each other miserable?"

At first, Lydia did not believe his words, but as his speech continued, she clearly was growing affected. Mr. Wickham's speech was quickly having an effect.

"I do not love you," he continued. "I never have, and never will. You chose to come, invited yourself, and you were meant to give me pleasure, no more than that. You are a fool, Lydia, a terrible fool! And I'm done entertaining your delusions. And do you want the real truth? I proposed to Elizabeth, and she rejected me. The only reason that I ever showed any attention to you was to get recompense for her slighting me. I never wanted you, I wanted her. And you are not her."

I closed my eyes. I had wanted Wickham to admit that he was never going to marry her, in hopes that it would lead to an awakening for Lydia.

Although, I never intended for him to tell her that he had initially chosen me.

I was driven from my thoughts when Lydia slapped Wickham across the face.

"You are evil!" Lydia cried.

"In some ways, so are you," he responded. "Now it's time that we see each other for what we truly are."

Lydia burst into tears and left the room.

"Well," Mr. Wickham said, "how did I do?"

"I didn't want you to tell her that you had proposed to me first," I said.

"You honestly think that speech was just for you, Miss Elizabeth?" Wickham questioned. "No. Part of it was for me and for her. I was speaking in frank honesty, for the first time in so long. As for your sister, one must be cruel to be kind. She needed to hear all that, or else she would never improve. When in Hertfordshire, I saw you attempt to improve her, with no success. You said that you would discharge all my debts and not seek retribution against me. I owed you this."

Breathing heavily, I was confused.

"Mr. Wickham," I concluded, "you have your freedom now. Please be a better man after this."

"We will see. I can give you no more promise than that."

With that, Colonel Forster led him out of the room. If all went well, then he would walk out of our lives forever.

"I should go to Lydia," I said, taking Mr. Darcy's arm. "She won't want to see me, but I have to try anyway."

"Understandable."

Colonel Forster took us to Mrs. Forster's room, where Lydia was weeping in Mrs. Forster's arms, and Mrs. Forster held her.

"Go away you both!" Lydia cried to us. We tried to reason with her, but she wanted nothing to do with us for a time.

"That was expected, I suppose," I said as we went back to the Grand Brighton. "Never fear, she will wake up tomorrow and begin to recover. That is the one gift we Bennet women were given: we can always recover."

Looking up at him, I was curious.

"How are you? After hearing Wickham speak, I am worried that you are affected by his confessions."

"I am disturbed by them. He lets his jealousies overwhelm him, leading to him committing vile actions, while also not seeing that he could never have run Pemberley or been the master of anyone. His desires are too selfish and insatiable."

"He would have ruined Pemberley, if he had been given your life."

"And yet, there is a part of me that wonders."

"Yes?" I asked.

"If I had listened to him before and talked him through his terrible phases, confronted the demons in him, he would have improved and not ever hurt anyone."

"I understand that way of thinking, but I would recommend not to believe that," I advised. "Some people are beyond being helped. Time teaches them to better themselves, more than any other lesson. Even if you had listened to him, I believe it all would have turned out the exact same way as it has. Or there is the chance that his behavior would have pulled you down with him. I wanted to believe he was a good man, and I want to believe that he will improve from this day, but I cannot control that. He controls himself. All that I can say is, when people choose to be villains, hear what they say, but never listen so much that you believe them. That's how they begin to work on you."

We reached our hotel.

"It's taking way too long for us to get married," he voiced.

"I know. This is agony."

CHAPTER 3

GROWTH OF CHARACTER

*A*ccording to the laws of balance, this recent tinge of scandal should have been repaid by there being no more calamities to be met with. We ought to have spent the rest of our time in Brighton with delight and ease. Truly, I had experienced enough dramatics to last me for a year.

"Give me boredom and consistency," I declared to Jane, Kitty, Georgiana, and Elena. "Anything but more of this."

Yet very little of our lives is spent getting what we wish, and I was no different from the rest of mankind. The Bingleys and Hursts had saved their outing for the next day and invited us again. This time, there was to be an addition to our party.

"We have stumbled upon another happy diversion," Mr. Bingley said. "I met Sir Aleck the other day, when walking, and invited him as well. Eagerly, he accepted, and he shall also be of our party."

Mr. Darcy accepted for us all, but Colonel Fitzwilliam had to return to spend that day in correspondence with the war office. For there was still the matter of where to place Mr. Martin and Mr. Wickham. Given Mr. Martin's reconciliation with Miss Elena, he could be positioned nearer to London, while Mr. Wickham was a more difficult dilemma. Colonel Forster did not want him to be in his regiment, and the Colonel had to bear in mind that our presence upset Wickham, and Wickham's presence upset us. The only suitable thing for all would be for Wickham to be banished to the Regulars, in a far-off county. Either way, that left Colonel Fitzwilliam having to spend the day sending out inquiries to find the perfect place to send Wickham.

As for Sir Aleck's company, I knew that Elena would be happy over it, but I was worried about Kitty.

"Never fear," Kitty assured me, "the sight of them together causes me pain, but I will never let them know of it. I shall just suffer in silence. And cry later."

My heart went out to her. Never in my life did I experience the painful sensation of being in the company of two people whose company caused me *that sort of* emotional disquiet. What I meant is that I never had a close friend who was being doted on by the man that I loved. Such a tangled web was not enjoyable to experience. I wondered how I would have dealt with it. If I were fortunate, I would have just laughed myself out of it.

With Colonel Fitzwilliam not being present, Mr. Bingley was at liberty to offer Jane his arm, and they walked among our company, speaking mostly to one another.

Sir Aleck was amiable and tried to include everyone in his attentions, but there was no way that he could continue to do so in Miss Elena's company. It was evident that he agreed to come because he wanted to see her, so he was unable to resist remaining at her side and growing to know her better. Indeed, they were very much in each other's confidence for a large portion of it.

That only left Mr. Darcy and Mr. Hurst to entertain Georgiana, Kitty, Mrs. Hurst, Miss Bingley, and myself. Mr. Hurst had his wife in one arm, Miss Bingley in another, and Mr. Darcy linked arms with me while Kitty and Georgiana walked arm in arm.

As we walked along the shoreline, we came upon some seaweed.

"Remarkable," Miss Bingley said, peering at it. "I have never seen seaweed before."

"Really?" Kitty asked. "I thought you would have, with your experience of the world. Elizabeth, Georgiana, Jane, and Elena, have you ever seen seaweed before?"

"We have not either," Jane said, "due to never going sea bathing, and only ever hearing of it in books."

"I did manage to see seaweed that was dried out and preserved," Elena explained. "My mother went sea bathing when I was a baby, and she brought some home, pressed. When I was a child, I would walk past where the seaweed was framed and wonder where she got it, what the sea was like, and my childlike mind took on a magical state. I viewed the sea as this fantastic place. Immediately, I wished that I was there."

"Much of our lives are spent," Sir Aleck observed, "wishing we were somewhere else than where we are."

"It is that age old saying of the grass being greener on the other side," I noted. "It leads to one always believing that someone has it better somewhere else."

"And while that may be very true," Kitty added, "for whenever we are saddened or crying, there must surely be another place where someone is laughing, it wonders how little we are happy where we are."

"It is the side effect to the human condition," Georgiana commented, "to always want something more than what we already have. We are bent on desiring more, which makes it all the more frightening when one does get everything that one wishes. For when you have reached the highest peak of the highest mountain, there is nowhere else to go but back down it."

"Oh, Miss Darcy," Mr. Hurst put in, "now I am disarmed. Once people begin to talk of the eternal tendencies of the human condition, I say that I am different, everyone else says you are not, I counterargue and say, 'I am', then they say, 'you are not'…and there's the end of it!"

We all laughed.

"And like you, Miss Bennets," Miss Bingley said, "our family does have a history of achieving one's fortune through trade."

"Our father was a manufacturer of textiles," Mrs. Hurst explained to Miss Elena. "He worked a great deal so that Charles could aspire to becoming a gentleman."

"I often forget that your family was in trade, like my mother's side of the family," I noted.

"Because sometimes even I forget it," Miss Bingley acknowledged, "and because of such, our parents were too busy to ever go sea-bathing. Faith, I do not even know if they ever went to a bathing place. Louisa, did mother and father ever mention if they went sea-bathing?"

"I do not recall them ever saying so," Mrs. Hurst answered. "They went to one of the bathing houses in Bath, but that's it." Her eyes widened with shock. "Our parents never came to the sea! Father could have done so when he was in America, however. He had to go there, a few times, for business as well as to see family."

"Family?" Jane asked, then she turned to Mr. Bingley. "You have family in America?"

Mr. Bingley looked confused.

"I never heard of such."

"It is not our brother's fault," Mrs. Hurst explained. "It was before he was born. Our father had cousins in America, but due to the colonies' revolution, both families became estranged from each other. You must understand that my father's cousins were born and raised here in Britain, but they moved to the colonies before the revolution began. At first, they were among the many people who were confused of which side to support when America and Britain began the war. They sympathized with both sides. This was the real truth behind the revolution of course. Too often it is described as extremes: either you were loyal to Britain, or you were a patriot to the colonies. Many people here in Britain and many in the colonies were both. They desired America to stay a part of Britain, but they understood the colonies' frustrations. You and Caroline had not been born when the war was still going on, so you didn't get the chance to see it. And it was right in the middle of the war that the rift in our family began."

"Began?" Georgiana asked. "Are you implying that the Bingleys in America eventually sided with the revolutionaries?"

"More British-born people fought alongside the colonists than people realize or wish to acknowledge," Mr. Hurst explained. "Just like quite a few Americans sided with us British. John Paul Jones and John Barry both were prominent in leading America's navy. The first was a Scotsman, and the second was an Irishman."

"Also," Sir Aleck added, "the man who helped finance the colonists' side of the war was named Robert Morris, who was born in England. England gave birth to the man who financially supported the colonists' armies. And when it comes to war, money is everything."

"Our father was always known for laughing at both America and Britain at the same time," I said. "He laughed at their uncouth ways, and our stiff ones, while also saying the joke was on all who misunderstood. For at the end of the day, it is too often forgotten that America's revolution was, to us, a civil war that was fought overseas. And we often argued about the names given to the war. I supported the names that the war is called, but Father called it the 'Most Confusing War of All Time'."

"One time I even heard him declare it as the 'Much Ado About Nothing' War," Kitty added with a chuckle. "Then afterwards he would grumble and say: 'except for all the times where it was legitimately about something!'"

Jane sighed. "Poor and dear Father, he could never really make up his mind about anything that was not philosophical. So, your family was split because of the war?" she asked the Bingleys again.

"Yes," Mrs. Hurst continued to narrate. "Our cousins eventually joined them. I was very little at the time, so I could easily get the names wrong, but I believe one of our cousins, Mr. Simon Bingley, did actually enlist and fight in the American army. I do believe that he even served under Benedict Arnold before Arnold changed sides. And another cousin of ours, Sally Bingley, became camp follower and a Molly Pitcher. If I am correct, a Molly Pitcher meant you were one of the women who would bring pitchers of water to the soldiers while they were fighting. It was a dangerous business, but the Bingleys in America eventually were known for being respected patriots, made even more respectable when the war was won.

"Our father never hated them for their decision. Like we've all established, it was a complicated war. He understood they were living amidst such strife and conflict, whereas he was separated from all that. Here in Britain, he was told of how the war was going, but our cousins were living in it. Between the rising taxes, the quartering of the British soldiers, King George's attitude towards them, the food shortages, the riots, the impressment, the tar and feathering of loyalists, all of it! Eventually, they had to choose a side, for the sake of all that was going on around them. Also, you have to recall that we were a family of trade. In America, families of trade were very respectable. Perhaps our cousins fought because it was the only place that they knew their children would be regarded as equal to everyone else."

"For all their defects," Sir Aleck explained, "that is their main virtue. The first time I went to America, from tavern women, to gravediggers, everyone spoke to me without fear or insecurity. It was surprising to me, at first, but eventually I grew to really like it. Also, I met people who were wealthy, but they were born poor. They acquired their fortune over the years and went into politics or became the most respected people of society. If the Bingleys in America were people of trade, then they had no choice. It was the best place to raise children if you are a family who needs to make their future, rather than their future already being made for them."

"What happened to your family when the war ended?" Kitty asked.

"The breach was permanent," Mrs. Hurst said, "because our father could not invite them to come to England, nor could he visit them. He had us to raise, and he wanted us to be respected in society. If rumor spread that he was entertaining his radical cousins who fought to break America from Britain, he would have been called out to spoil. I suppose that he sacrificed so much for us."

Mr. Bingley looked stunned. "And he never told me this? Or Caroline? I wish that he had. Now I feel more indebted to him than ever, but because he's gone, I can't tell him."

"I am certain that he knows," Jane assured him.

"And in either case," Mr. Hurst said, "he couldn't tell you. Your father was a man, cut from the very same cloth that we are cut from; there are some things we should talk about, but we are told not to."

"Very true," Mr. Darcy confirmed, "sadly, very true."

"What a conversation," I considered, "and it all started with seaweed."

Eventually, we returned to the hotel, dining with each other.

"What do you think?" Kitty asked. "A story about a romance between a soldier and a woman during a war? I had been thinking of it for some time, but I didn't know if it would be a good idea. What do you think?"

We all confirmed that it would be marvelous and began to offer suggestions with alacrity. Kitty tolerated our suggestions with equanimity, but I knew that she would decide what she wished.

Our eagerness to talk about it, helped distract her from seeing that Sir Aleck was falling in love with Miss Elena more and more by the moment.

All of us were on a similar path, however, where there was growth of character on all sides.

Mr. Darcy and I finally were able to move on from any storm clouds that rested over our heads before.

Elena was homeless, and ironically, this was the happiest state that she could be in. Even more, she was seeing that there was life after a lost first love. Her past was not a shadow that was hanging over her, and she learned not to let her spirit fall into self-pity. Elena had quickly learned a lesson that it took most of us humans' years to learn: to move on.

She was not alone in this journey. Kitty, who once was envious of the path of others, wishing for attention herself, learned to leave the table when love was not being served to her. She was learning to smile when facing reality was hard to do and suffer her heartache without saying a word.

Sir Aleck was learning what it was like to consider leaving behind his title of being 'the legendary and penultimate bachelor'. He had been perfectly happy with this title for so long, as Darcy had told me, that he didn't ever see himself as being anything more than the person that everyone came to for advice, because he was free from everything. But no one is ever fully free. And Sir Aleck was now learning that lesson, the hard way.

Mr. and Mrs. Hurst were learning to be less critical, less heartless in their judgments on others, and were becoming more human. They seemed to be more able to forgive the rest of the world for not being on their level and seemed to be willing to relinquish their snobbish nature.

Mr. Hurst realized that it was not uncouth to speak.

Georgiana was growing comfortable in her skin, and even was beginning to sing in public.

Mr. Bingley had given into the reality that he had to be patient and accept whatever choice that Jane must make. After all, his actions were the reason that everything had occurred the way it had between them.

Jane knew that she didn't have to choose anymore. The answer would present itself over time—or one of them would get bored in chasing after her if she were lucky.

And Mama and Mary knew that we would soon come home.

CHAPTER 4

ANOTHER DAY, ANOTHER IMPEDIMENT

The next day was supposed to be the day before our departure, and we were going to visit Lydia. Georgiana, Kitty, and Elena came to our room because they needed more help with their hair. They all chose to have the same hairstyle, with a certain type of braid.

"It had been my idea," Elena suggested, "but the servants have no idea of how to do it."

"And so, I suggested you both," Kitty said. "I told them how you and Jane know how to do it correctly."

"Oh, I remember the hairstyle," Jane said. "You three would look so adorable like that."

"That is what we hope," Georgiana said. They were all about to sit down when Georgiana saw something out of the window.

"What is it?" I asked her.

"I think I know that carriage." She went to the window and looked out. "Yes, I do! Elizabeth, my Aunt Catherine de Bourgh is here!"

I felt my stomach turn to lead.

"Are you certain?" I asked, although I was afraid it was true.

"Yes, I am sure of it. Yes, there she is."

"Your aunt?" Elena asked. "Now I am very curious!"

She and Kitty also went to the window, but Jane saw the horror etched on my face.

"Eliza? What's wrong?"

"You don't know this," I professed, "but Lady Catherine de Bourgh had intended Mr. Darcy to marry her daughter, Anne de Bourgh."

Seeing what I meant, Jane's eyes also widened.

"Oh. And does she know that you and Mr. Darcy are engaged?"

"I might have mentioned it in a letter to Charlotte. It was only right to do so. I didn't think or consider that she would tell Lady Catherine or how the great lady would take the news."

"You do not think she would be upset because Mr. Darcy chose to marry someone he loved? After all, he is her nephew."

I gave her a look.

"From the little that I know about Lady Catherine, she is not the sort to come all this way to offer her well-wishes."

I left the room and knocked on Mr. Darcy's door. Soon, he opened it and he was still in his shirtsleeves.

"Why do you not look happy?" he asked when seeing my face. "I don't want to hear any bad news."

"But we might see it. Lady Catherine de Bourgh is here."

Mr. Darcy's face froze, and he quickly understood the gravity of the matter.

"What? Where?"

"We saw her from out of our window. There's no mistaking it. Your aunt-mother has come to Brighton. I just wanted to know, how dear is your aunt's wish for you to marry your cousin?"

"Very much. Call it practical or cowardice, but I have been putting off telling her. We are fortunate that this shall happen in so public a place."

"Why?"

"With any luck, my aunt will make less noise."

He put on his jacket, and he, Georgiana and I went down to the first floor and soon were met by Lady Catherine being tended to by much of the hotel's staff. Her luggage was being brought in and carried to one of the largest rooms in the place, making it evident that she had come to stay for some time.

First, she didn't see us, but we saw her barking orders to those who tended to her.

"There is no point in us going to her," Mr. Darcy said, "she will see us eventually."

Still, we stood there.

Then, out of the corner of her eye, she beheld us. It was like watching a wolf's hair prickling along its back, sensing that it was not alone, then it turned around and faced its inspector.

That was how it felt when she turned and looked at us. First, she saw Darcy, then Georgiana, and at last, her eyes fell on me, and they turned into slits.

"And now she's seen us," I commented. "I wonder what will happen next."

"We'll see," Darcy responded, and we all approached her. "Aunt Catherine, it is a remarkable surprise to see you here."

"Yes," Georgiana added, "but it is a pleasure."

"Lady Catherine," I added, "I echo the sentiments that your niece and nephew feel."

"My coming is most important and whether you shall receive any pleasure from what I have to say will be entirely up to you. For I do not come to give you all pleasure."

"Might I invite you to my quarters while your room is being prepared?" Mr. Darcy asked civilly. "For we are quite in public."

"I choose where our conversation will take place, and not you. We will go to your quarters because I believe it to be the proper place."

I looked at Mr. Darcy and saw his jaw tighten at her impertinence.

"Very well," he responded, "let us go."

"What floor are you staying on?"

"The second floor."

"Foolish! You should have stayed on the ground floor."

Moving before us, she walked up the steps and we had to follow her, despite that she didn't know what room Mr. Darcy had. When reaching the second level, she gave Mr. Darcy a sharp look.

"Follow me," he said, going to his room. She followed us there, her posture tall, erect, and she appeared as if she was a queen who was walking to her throne to announce a beheading.

When she entered the room, and Darcy shut the door behind her, he offered to order some refreshments.

"No," Lady Catherine said, sitting down in the prominent seat of the room. "I do not expect to be here for long, because I will immediately carry my point and expect to be satisfied."

"What could you be talking of Aunt?" Georgiana asked.

"What is evident to all in the room, except you, I suppose," she snapped. She turned and looked at how Mr. Darcy and I were standing in close proximity of each other and made the correct assumption.

"When seeing you both at Rosings together, if I had known what it would lead to, I would have cast you out of Kent immediately, Miss Bennet."

"You control all of Kent?" I asked, not alarmed.

"My power is greater than you think."

"I will ask you not to insult my fiancée, aunt," Mr. Darcy countered. "I will not stand for that."

When hearing him call me thus, her eyes raised.

"You call her your fiancée?"

"I do."

"Then you can be of no loss in understanding why I have come."

"On the contrary," I responded, playing coy, "I cannot fully assume what has driven you all this way. What would your ladyship propose by it?"

"You are pretending to feign ignorance, and that is a waste of time. A most alarming report has reached Rosings Park, of your intended elopement to each other. Upon hearing this report, I instantly set off to make my opinion known."

"And this is where you do not give us your blessing," I noted.

"Miss Bennet, you know better than to trifle with me. It is bad enough that I had to endure hearing such a repulsive rumor, but I knew to be practical and wise, as my character has often been praised for. Immediately, I declared it to be a scandalous falsehood, circulated by you, Miss Bennet, and had no veracity to it at all. But now, I am here, and I find all sense to be abandoned, because what ought to be false, now appears to be true."

"It is," Mr. Darcy said. "I have become attached to the most perfect woman that I have ever encountered. Not only has she proven to be the precise sort of woman for me, but also a very good friend to Georgiana. Aunt, I would ask that you offer me your well-wishes."

"Offer you my well-wishes!" she repeated, growing more enraged by the minute. "Fitzwilliam, have you lost your senses?"

"I do believe that I am in possession of my full faculties."

"And I would thank you not to criticize my fiancé's intelligence," I supported, "for you are very much out of line."

"This will not be born," she continued. "Fitzwilliam, you are engaged to my daughter! You know that you are intended for Anne."

"When was that intention ever uttered from my lips?" he asked. "When have I ever confirmed that I wished to pursue this plan?"

"Your confirmation was never needed. It was every day implied from the arrangement that your mother and I set about when you and my daughter were born. Are you so insensitive to the chief wishes of her? I thought you were a man who loved your mother."

"I am," he repeated, his voice hollow from rage. "Do not ever presume me to not care about her."

"Aunt, that was very unfair," Georgiana cut in. "You know that Fitzwilliam loved Mama terribly and cried when she died."

I looked at Mr. Darcy, surprised by this news. It was natural for anyone to weep when losing their mother, but to see Mr. Darcy cry was another matter entirely.

"And that's why I call upon his duty to remember that he respected her," Lady Catherine continued, knowing to play on Darcy's weakness to his mother's memory. "Fitzwilliam, your mother's dying wish was to see Pemberley and Rosings Park connected. Bonding two estates of the North and the South in the most perfect union. Such a connection would make you almost like a prince of the aristocracy. It has all the credit and benefit of a proper arrangement. Perhaps in this moment,

Fitzwilliam, you have been driven in by this lady's arts and allurements, and you have forgotten what you owe to your family and to yourself."

"My parents worked hard to raise Georgiana and me in the proper way, and I thank them," Darcy countered. "Truly, I thank them every day of my life. But that is where it ends, because if Mother's dying wish was for me to marry a woman who I did not love, then she was not my mother. But I know that my mother would have preferred me to make an arrangement based on my happiness, rather than my wife's pocketbook."

He glared at her. "You forget the woman that your sister was. My mother did not marry my father just because of Pemberley. She didn't even know that he was the eldest son, and heir of Pemberley, until after she had given Father a lock of her hair. All that she knew was that she liked him, and then when he revealed his wealth, she knew that the match would be welcome by her parents. If she had seen the man that I grew up to be, and the woman that Anne has grown up to be, then she would know that I am the last man in the world who could make her happy. Aunt, you cannot deny that Anne does not feel any congenial feelings to me."

"What have her feelings to do with it?"

"It has everything to do with it," Georgiana reproved. "Aunt Catherine, Anne is your daughter. Surely, you must think of her happiness now."

"I am thinking of her happiness now," Lady Catherine bellowed, "for I would not be here if I were not so. I am thinking of her future, her welfare, and her life when I am gone."

"If you cared for her," I said, "then why aren't you asking her what would make her happy? Right now, you are speaking for her and planning her life for her. If she is to be the heiress of Rosings Park, then how can she be if you never let her make any decisions, even pertaining to her own life?"

Her nose in the air, she replied, "Young people need guidance."

"But they also need someone to encourage them to lift up their voice and support their own thoughts and feelings. You do not let Anne do such."

"I will not be lectured by you on parenting, Miss Bennet, the most unfeeling and selfish girl that I have ever met. I have more experience in the matter and have often been praised for being an ideal parent. I am above reproach in that regard. Fitzwilliam, I order you one last time to quit this foolish decision, end this improper engagement, and come to your senses."

"I will do no such thing, Aunt. That would be a crime against my heart, and against Elizabeth. I have promised myself to her, and to that I hold."

When seeing that she could not sway Mr. Darcy's good opinion of me, Lady Catherine was resigned and turned to me again. After her repeated offenses toward me, I wondered that she would think I would listen to anything else that she had to say.

"Then one last time, I will appeal to you, Miss Bennet," she said. "I would advise you not to quick the sphere to which you were brought up."

"In marrying your nephew, I would not regard myself as quitting that sphere," I argued. "He is a gentleman, and I am a gentleman's daughter."

"But who is your mother? Who are your aunts and uncles? Do not think me ignorant of them. Is this to be the family that my nephew connects himself to? It shall not be endured."

"If my relations are questionable just because they are people who gather their wealth from trade, then I am happy to be guilty of having such family members. There is something very wrong with a world that ridicules others for working for a living."

"This is your belief!" she replied, scandalized. "Such a horrible sentiment." Taking a step closer to me, she continued. "Do you know what will happen if you continue with this vulgar arrangement? You will make my nephew a humiliation to the world, and you will watch as your marriage will expose each to the contempt of society. And when that happens, do you think that he will love you anymore? No, he will look on you with contempt, for you were the means through which his life was ruined. Your alliance would be a disgrace. Your name would never be mentioned by any of us."

"These are heavy misfortunes indeed," I replied, evenly. "But as long as I have Darcy's love, I do not care about the rest. There are too many benefits and joys of becoming Mrs. Darcy that would override any feelings of loss that you have mentioned."

"And they will stay as such," Mr. Darcy said. "If you threaten my fiancée once more, Aunt, with such offensive terms, then I shall remove you from my life. I love you, but not so much that I will allow you to belittle and berate the woman that I am happy to spend the rest of my life with. As for this moment, I am asking you to leave of your own free will."

"If you marry her, Fitzwilliam, then the shades of Pemberley will be thus polluted with her presence."

"That is enough!" Mr. Darcy roared, in a way that frightened anyone who would dare oppose him. Lady Catherine flinched, taken aback. "Aunt, remove yourself from my room. Never come near Elizabeth again, or I will forcefully remove you from her company. You have polluted this scene enough with your imprudent manner."

So intimidated by his tone, Lady Catherine was silenced. She walked to the door, placed her hand on the knob, and then she gave one final quiet word.

"Do you know why I want you to marry my daughter, Fitzwilliam?" she asked. "It is because my daughter is frail and meek. She does not have the strength or ability to run a household like Rosings Park. I talk for her because she has no notion of how to speak for herself. I fear that any man she marries might take advantage of her, because she will not fight. I planned your marriage with your mother when you were infants, because it was a romantic idea. But as you aged, and showed your steadiness, your sturdiness, your reliability, and your ability to care for Georgiana, I knew that you would be the perfect man to protect Anne. You were not vicious, abusive, or manipulative. I knew that you would be Anne's shield. And now, there is no chance of that. Now, I do not know who can save my daughter."

This confession surprised us, and we were humbled. It didn't eradicate our memory of her offensive words to us, but it did put things into another perspective.

"Aunt," Georgiana said at last, "these are heavy confessions you give, and they would have garnered sympathy before. Yet, you said this after hurting Elizabeth and Fitzwilliam. Also, you cannot fully be sure. If you were to give Anne more power over her life, then she might surprise you."

"You don't know what it's like to be a mother to a meek child. None of you know. I shall remain here for three more days before departing. Fitzwilliam, I hope that you have come to your senses by then."

At last, she left us alone.

———

"She really said all of that?" Jane asked me as all of us women sat in my room. Georgiana and I had finished telling them all that happened, and they all were aghast.

"Yes, she did," I confirmed.

"I do not know whether to give her a broom for her to ride on, for she is witch-like," Kitty said, "or to offer her a shoulder to cry on. Then again, she seems too proud to cry, the demonic cretin that she is."

"Believe me," Georgiana said, "she may have felt that my brother was a good guardian for Anne, but that was an addition. Ultimately, it still has to do with wealth and the desire for control. I am sorry for her, but that's where it ends."

"So," I queried, "I should not feel bad for remaining fast to loving your brother?"

"Of course not." Georgiana pressed, taking my hand. "Do not let her influence you in that way. I love my aunt, but she would have said anything to make you and my brother doubt each other's bond. Do not let her affect you in that way."

I rubbed my fingers over my face. "Normally I would not. She just caught me in a moment of weakness. I cannot deny that I wish to go to Darcy now, to make sure that he feels the same way that I do."

"Which reminds me," Jane said, "you need a moment alone for some time. Georgiana, Kitty and Elena, I still have to do your hair. Never fear, I can do it all myself. Let us go to your room and let Lizzy to herself."

They all agreed to this and prepared to go to Kitty's room. Before exiting, Jane turned to me.

"And Eliza? When I return, I shall take some time to check for spiders again. It may take quite a few minutes."

Giving me a knowing look, she closed the door behind her.

"Jane," I said to the air, "you are the greatest sister in the world."

Going to Mr. Darcy's door, I knocked on it. Shortly, Mr. Darcy opened it and he relaxed when he saw me.

"Worried that I was your formidable aunt?" I asked.

"Yes, I was."

"Is there any chance that you are willing to let your fiancée into your room?"

He looked at the hallway and back at me.

"Where is Jane?"

"Making sure to be everywhere else but where a proper chaperone should be. God bless her."

"Yes, god bless her indeed," he said. Instinctively, I reached my hand out to him.

"Will you take my hand?"

Slowly, he did so, then he pulled me into the room, closing the door behind him.

"I just wanted you to know…"

"Yes?" he questioned.

"That I love you more than life itself. I am aware that you have sacrificed so much for me, that I am indebted to you, and that the only way that I can repay you is by promising to never stop loving you, till the day that I die."

"Say no more of that!" he professed, grabbing my dress and pulling me to him. He closed the space between us, pressed his lips against mine, and lifted me up. I fell into his embrace.

He carried me over to the sofa and sat down with me on his lap. Rather than ceasing, we continued our passionate act for a duration, and he placed his hands along my neck. Gradually, he ran his hand down my throat and let it rest along the top of my dress. Slowly, he ran his hands along the front of my gown, and at last lowered his hands inside of it. I could not resist letting a moan escape me as I felt the pleasure of his hands along my breasts. Gradually, he ran his other hand under my dress, lifting the bottom of it and sliding his fingers up my thighs. At last, he reached the top and drove his fingers in between my thighs.

"I love you," I cried. "I really do."

"And I love you. We must marry soon. I cannot stand much more of this!"

"I know. After we return Lydia to Longbourn, let's immediately go to Pemberley and get married there."

"Yes. But for now…"

He carried me towards the bed.

Someone knocking at the door stopped us.

"I have checked my room, Mr. Darcy," Jane said, "and there are no spiders to be seen."

"Are you sure?" I whispered, more out of frustration rather than out of a desire for her to hear.

"This is the most painful timing of my life," Mr. Darcy groaned.

"Our lives," I said. "Believe me. *Our* lives."

He had to set me down. I straightened myself and I went to the door. Opening it, Jane and I checked to make sure that there was no one to spy on me as I tiptoed out of Darcy's room and rushed into mine.

When we were alone, I turned to Jane.

"You save me from myself," I praised her.

"I do what I can," Jane responded with a wry smile.

———

That evening, we dined with the Bingleys, Hursts, Colonel Fitzwilliam and Sir Aleck again. This time, it was even more evident that Sir Aleck was in love, for he and Elena sat next to each other and spoke to no one else the entire evening.

"Tell me more about your writing, Miss Kitty?" Mr. Hurst said. "How goes your novel?"

"Oh, I have finished it," Kitty said, "and have begun writing the next one. This one is inspired by our discussion that we had as we were walking along the shore yesterday. It shall be called Romance & Revolution. It is about a romance between a man and woman who are on two opposing sides of a war. The man is a colonel in the army, and the woman is a patriot to the other side. I have yet to determine if it will be the American Revolution or not."

"A romance with a soldier?" Colonel Fitzwilliam perked up. "Really?"

"Never fear," Kitty said, "you are safe from my pen, Colonel. I will make certain not to force you into being my model for it."

"I do not know whether to be happy or sad over that," Colonel Fitzwilliam chuckled. "Should I be happy that I am not your subject, or sad that I am not worthy to be your subject?"

"You are worthy," she encouraged him, "but I do not want you to feel as if you are the constant center of a joke. The story will be both comedic as well as serious, as well as tragic. What if you don't like to fall on either of those sides?"

"I am all three of those sides. I would be unrealistic to pretend to be otherwise."

"Colonel, you sound as if you wish to be immortalized. I can very well understand that intention, but there is one drawback to it all."

"What is that?"

"That I may never be published!"

We all laughed.

"I must be realistic, despite it all," Kitty continued, "for how often are us female writers, who are writing books of little information, but all sentiment, ever regarded? If we women are not serious and lecturing the rest of womankind on how we could be better wives, then our words are not worth much. Therefore, if you are wishing to live forever through a character, dear Colonel, then I am the worst writer that you can find."

"Leave it to me to decide if you are the worst," he responded, "and I believe that you are not. As much as this is insensitive to your own sex, please believe that I advise this simply out of consideration for your success."

"Are you about to propose that I take up a male name?"

"Oh, you anticipated my suggestion."

"I had thought of it. But a male name, of obscurity, is actually as worthless as a woman's name. That is the one way in which we are equal. If men and women are equally poor and not noteworthy." She bit into her food and then her face looked up, shocked.

"Kitty?" I asked.

"It is nothing. Well, actually, it is something! Colonel, I may have considered this option before, but us speaking of it now has led to me seeing things in a different light. I think I may have an idea."

"Pray tell us," Elena said, "what is it?"

"I will tell you once I have any hope of succeeding," Kitty said, "but until then, I shall keep it to myself."

We all ate on.

———

We parted ways at the end of the evening, content that everyone was beginning to feel like friends. All seemed as if it was falling into place as we went to our room, with Colonel Fitzwilliam escorting us there as well, wishing for a quick moment with Jane. As we reached the second landing, we were quickly come upon by Lady Catherine de Bourgh.

"Aunt?" Mr. Darcy began.

"Fitzwilliam! I must speak with you."

"I will have no more of you offending Miss Elizabeth."

"It is not that," she rushed out, her face white with hysterics. "It is something else. I need to speak with you and Richard."

In her hand, there was a letter, and I presumed that it was the root of her distress.

"Aunt, whatever is the matter?" Colonel Fitzwilliam asked.

"We cannot talk of it here. Please, we must speak in my quarters. This is not a matter to speak about on the stairs."

"Very well," Darcy said, ushering us forth.

"I will not have any of *them* come!" she snapped, referring to us Bennets and Elena.

"They will come, or I will not."

"Lady Catherine," I urged, "you appear to be in distress. So, would it not be beneficial for you to not slight the people who are coming to help you? In more colloquial terms, beggars can't be choosers right now."

She looked at me, resentful.

"Very well, since I have no choice, all come and hurry."

We proceeded to follow her to her room, and once we entered, the change was immediate.

Now that she was no longer in public, Lady Catherine's 'imposing' demeanor broke down and she sat in a chair, beginning to weep.

"Aunt Catherine?" Darcy asked, affected.

"Aunt," Colonel Fitzwilliam said, rushing to her side and caressing her arm. "What is it? Tell us so that we can share this sorrow."

"It is Anne."

"What has happened to her?" I asked.

"She has eloped."

CHAPTER 5

JUST WHEN EVERYTHING WAS COMING TOGETHER

*W*e all stood there, absolutely stunned.

"Anne?" I repeated. "Anne de Bourgh has eloped?"

"No, she hasn't," Lady Catherine denied, "I know that she hasn't. This must be a scandalous falsehood. Of course, it is. Charlotte Collins simply has heard a false rumor. My Anne is far too intelligent to do such a thing. She would not hurt me so. No, I know that it is all lies."

"Aunt," Darcy dissuaded, "I understand what you are going through now, which is initial denial. That's how most of these circumstances begin. But if you really believed that this was a lie, then you would not be so overturned now."

"And I know Charlotte," I said, stepping forward. "Ma'am, she would not say such a thing unless it was true." I looked at her hand. "Is that letter from Charlotte?"

"Yes."

Colonel Fitzwilliam placed his hand on the letter.

"Aunt, would you please let me read the letter, so that we all might have the pleasure of understanding better?"

"We must move quickly," Aunt Catherine said, in a bit of a daze as she handed the letter to the Colonel. "Or it will be too late."

Taking the letter, Colonel Fitzwilliam began to read it aloud.

Dear Lady Catherine,

I write this letter with the worst of news to give you, and it is with a heavy heart that I must tell you that Mrs. Jenkinson and I woke up this morning to find Anne de Bourgh missing. She did not come down to breakfast, and the servants quickly reported that she was not in her room but found a letter on her desk.

Upon opening it, Anne informed us all that she had eloped in the dead of night and had thrown herself fully into the power of Mr. Orwell, our clergyman. I have immediately called down at the parsonage, his servants all had not seen him since the day before, I have also sent servants on the road to Gretna Green to try and overtake them.

However, since Mr. Orwell and Anne have had such an advantage, they might not be recaptured in time. I fear that maybe my efforts are too late.

I recognize that, in your eyes, I have failed as a companion, and I will resign my post immediately. I am heartily sorry for not being more attentive. But please believe, like all these matters usually are, the rest of us were quite left in the dark, and Anne's plan were kept secret very well.

I wish that I wrote to give you better news. We hope to see you return to Rosings as soon as you receive this letter, to be here to receive your daughter and her new husband when she arrives home again.

Yours etc.
Charlotte Collins

"Mrs. Collins did a terrible job of being her companion, indeed!" Lady Catherine cried. "I shall make her quit the house immediately when I return."

"This wasn't Charlotte's fault," Jane put in.

"She should have watched Anne more closely!"

"How does that change the fact that you didn't?" Kitty asked.

Lady Catherine looked as if she had been slapped across the face.

"How dare you speak to me in such a way?! You are all beneath me."

"They are not," I argued, not willing to let her arrogance flare up. "They just wish for you to see the point and purpose of your own actions. Don't you see that the *only* way that your daughter had the chance to elope was because you had left Rosings Park to come to Brighton and lecture Mr. Darcy on not accepting your daughter. All of this happened because you chose to intervene on your nephew's happiness."

"If he had done his duty and married Anne, then I never would have needed to come here in the first place."

"That is neither here nor there, since it is evident that Anne never wanted to marry me," Mr. Darcy said, his tone gentle. He was not trying to berate her, but just to make her see reasons. "Aunt, don't you see? Anne eloped with this clergyman because she knew that you would never accept the match. You came here with a desire to persuade me to abandon Elizabeth, when all the while Anne was in love with someone else. You came all this way for a marriage that would never have happened. And thus, you brought about the means through which Anne could make her great escape. You brought about your own self-defeating prophecy."

"Is that why you are here? To lecture me!"

"No. I am here to offer our company in taking you back to Rosings. If there is no word from Anne when we get there, we shall set out to Gretna Green ourselves to find what has become of them. But for me to do so, then I will only come to offer you company and counsel if you accept Elizabeth as my future bride, and her family as our family—respecting them from thenceforth. For right now, *our* family are the ones who are the more scandalous connection. Your plans for me to marry Anne have been destroyed by Anne herself. You must let that dream go."

Lady Catherine covered her mouth with her handkerchief and looked at the fire in the hearth.

"How did it come to this?" she asked, still looking at the fire. "How did I lose everything?"

"You have lost nothing, but hopefully just gained a new son-in-law."

"And what sort of man is this Mr. Orwell?" Colonel Fitzwilliam asked. "For a clergyman to elope does not cast him in a favorable light."

"Charlotte referred to him as a good man that Anne trusted," I noted. "But we don't know what sort of man he is."

"He is a villain, and he has been thriving like a viper in my bosom," Lady Catherine hissed. "He was a fortune hunter the entire time."

"That may be true," Mr. Darcy confirmed. "We must all prepare ourselves to leave by the end of two hours."

"Do you think we should ask Mr. Bingley to come?" Kitty asked. "For if you all need to search for them, ultimately, then three gentlemen are better than two."

Colonel Fitzwilliam looked to Jane, instinctively wondering if she agreed to this idea.

"That is a very good point," Jane admitted, "and it would help. For, if we leave the Bingleys so suddenly, then it would look too indelicate."

"That's true," I said, not wishing to delay. "Now, I just need to go to Colonel Forster and retrieve Lydia."

"Lydia won't come easily," Kitty said. "I'll come with you."

"Good. Now, we have not a moment to lose."

With all the speed of people with a purpose, we arranged everything. Mr. Darcy had gone off to appeal to Mr. Bingley to come along, Jane finished packing my things while Georgiana and Elena did the same, and Colonel Fitzwilliam escorted us.

When going to the Forsters, we were met by Mrs. Forster, who had greeted us warmly.

"I know that I must not appear to you all as the best companion," she began, "but I truly do feel remorse over Lydia's plight. I should have watched her closely and marked her feelings for Wickham as being more than a passing fancy."

"Thank you," I said, "but say no more of that. We harbor no ill will toward you, but merely came to retrieve Lydia. We have to leave today, and we need her to come a couple hours sooner than we decided."

She lowered her voice and continued.

"She is in her room. She has been a little sullen. I love your sister, but now I regret ever inviting her."

"Thank you." I turned to the Colonel. "Hopefully, we shall not be long."

He waited in the dining parlor with Mrs. Forster while Kitty and I went to Lydia's room.

"Lydia?" Kitty called as she knocked.

"Kitty, what is it?" Lydia called from the other side.

"I am here with Lizzy. We have to leave a couple hours sooner than we hoped, so we've come to help you pack."

"Tell Lizzy to go away."

Kitty looked at me.

"We don't have time for this, do we?" she asked.

"No, we don't."

I turned the knob and opened the door to see Lydia look at me, incredulous.

"Had a feeling that there was no lock on this door," I observed.

"I am not speaking to you!" Lydia wailed.

"Good," Kitty said, closing the door behind us. "Then that means that you can just listen. Lydia, we need to leave now, so we will help you pack your things so that we can be gone sooner."

"Why should I go anywhere with you?!"

"Because we are your sisters, you idiot!" Kitty bellowed, much to Lydia's surprise. And mine as well.

"Kitty, why are you treating me thus? We are the best of friends!"

"If we were, then you would not have thought to elope and put our family in the worst situation imaginable. You didn't think about us when you were off, ready to throw your maidenhead aside so casually. Let us be honest here. You are angry because you were foolish enough to run off with a man that had no reason to marry you, because your love for him blinded you from the fact that he obviously liked Lizzy—truly, how did you not see that? And then, when your family saved you from the clutches of this pernicious monster, you hate us because we cared for you? Because Mr. Darcy, the Colonel and Elizabeth saved you?"

"Kitty, leave me alone."

Kitty grabbed Lydia's hands and pulled her toward her, forcing Lydia to look into her eyes.

"I know why you want us to leave you alone," Kitty hissed. "It's because you are embarrassed. It's because you hate us for seeing you fail at something, for seeing you be unsuccessful at winning a man's heart. Well, that is part of growing older; getting your heart broken is inevitable, and sometimes, others are going to see that occur. Shame sometimes happens publicly, and perhaps it is good that it does, because it makes us work to not put ourselves in that situation again. But here's the thing: no one did this to you, but yourself. And that's what scares you above all. Now you must look at yourself in the mirror and see what you really are. And you can't stand the sight of yourself now because it will force you to realize that you took a wrong step somewhere. It will make you feel as if you have to change and improve yourself. Well, here is the truth. You do need to change and improve so that this never happens again. You need to see your shame now because that is how you begin."

Lydia began to weep, pushed herself away from Kitty, collapsed on the bed and cried into her pillow.

"And we need your help," Kitty continued. "Another woman is in danger now. We must go and help her. The sooner that you get packed, the sooner we can go and help this woman. So doing as we say can help you recover. We'll give you five minutes to have your cry out."

Kitty gave me a look, and we left the room.

"How…" I began, at a loss for how to phrase everything. "I did not know that you knew how to speak like that."

"It was more acting than anything else," she confessed. "In my last book, I wrote two sisters who had a similar argument, so I applied that situation to this one."

We joined Mrs. Forster and the Colonel in the parlor and told them that Lydia needed a few minutes to collect herself. After five minutes rose and fell, Kitty and I went back into the room and saw

Lydia still laying on the bed, forlorn.

"I should have foreseen that," Kitty admitted.

"No one is perfect," I said, unmoved and not perturbed. "We'll just have to pack for her."

We packed for Lydia as she remained on the bed. We managed to finish within a quarter of an hour and the only thing that remained was for us to move Lydia.

"Lydia," I intoned, "we need you to get up now."

"I don't want to move," Lydia voiced, depressed. "I never want to leave this spot. I want to die here."

"I cannot stand such dramatics at a time like this," I said, going over to her bed. I lifted up one side of the mattress, Lydia rolled off it, and then fell on the floor.

"What did you do?" Lydia cried, standing up, angry.

"You are moving now."

"Well, I won't leave this spot."

Suddenly, Mrs. Forster entered with a pitcher and a cup in her hand. She dipped the cup in the water, then splashed the cup of water at Lydia.

Lydia wailed loudly enough to wake the dead.

"Your sisters have come to get you, so you are going! Now move! Keep moving! Keep moving!" Mrs. Forster said, taking another cupful and hurling it at Lydia. With each cupful, Lydia moved toward the door, as Colonel Fitzwilliam, Kitty and I picked up her bags and followed them out.

As we did so, Colonel Fitzwilliam and Kitty accidentally bumped elbows with each other.

"Colonel," Kitty apologized, "I am sorry for all the incidents that have occurred in your life since we entered it. I can very well understand if you cannot bear the sight of us for much longer."

"On the contrary," Colonel Fitzwilliam assured her, "I cannot explain why, but I have never felt more alive than when I am around your family."

Kitty smiled.

"It is always nice to carry luggage next to a man who always knows the right thing to say."

Colonel Fitzwilliam laughed.

In a couple hours we all were assembled and leaving for Kent. In one carriage, Lady Catherine sat with Colonel Fitzwilliam and Georgiana. In the other carriage, all four of us Bennet sisters and Elena were seated.

Mr. Darcy and Mr. Bingley were riding alongside us on horseback.

As they did so, Mr. Bingley smiled at Jane through the carriage window.

"Well," I said to Elena, "we have put you through a series of events."

"No apology is necessary," Elena said merrily. "I am having the time of my life."

CHAPTER 6

HOME LEFT BEHIND, THE WORLD AHEAD

*L*eaving Brighton was the easiest thing in the world. While we did enjoy the delights of the bathing-place, except that it was too cold to go sea-bathing, we had seen and experienced enough to make us all exhausted.

We broke our journey at an inn that was along the road, but eventually, we arrived at Rosings Park. Charlotte eagerly met us once the carriage arrived, followed by Mrs. Jenkinson and other servants who attended to Lady Catherine immediately.

Lady Catherine marched past Charlotte and Mrs. Jenkinson because she still felt contempt for them. When seeing us Bennets, however, Charlotte felt lighter and rushed to us.

"I never thought to see your face during this time," she cried as she embraced me. "I am glad to see you all."

Then she embraced Jane, Kitty and Lydia as well.

"You do not know the comfort of seeing your faces here."

"We are happy to help in whatever way we can," I assured her. "There, you see? You are not alone now." I turned to Mrs. Jenkinson. "Mrs. Jenkinson, these are my sisters, Miss Jane Bennet, Miss Kitty and Miss Lydia."

Mrs. Jenkinson met us with more kindness and amicability than she had when I first met her. To be sure, she now needed us, so I became more important.

"Charlotte," I asked as we entered, "has there been any good word from Anne and Mr. Orwell?"

"Yes, there has. Mrs. Jenkinson and I received a letter from them this morning."

"It is as we feared," Mrs. Jenkinson said to all of us as the servants took our cloaks and bonnets in the vestibule. "They are married."

Taking Lydia's arm, I whispered to her. "Lydia, please, for all our sakes, listen to what is happening, but don't say anything during it. Lady Catherine won't understand your humor. Also, do not repeat a thing that is said here today."

"Let me see if I got this all right," she retorted. "You are ashamed of me."

"No, I am not. I just need you to promise me this."

"Very well," she said stiffly. "I won't say anything to her."

When we entered, Lady Catherine sat down in the sitting room and ordered for some tea and cakes to be brought out.

"I may be amid turmoil," Lady Catherine announced as we all sat down, "but let it not be said that I lost my manners of propriety and proper protocol."

Charlotte and Mrs. Jenkinson entered like mice who were trembling before a cat.

"Don't slouch, you both!" Lady Catherine snapped at them. "You'll make me despise the sight of you both more than I do already."

"Lady Catherine," Charlotte began, "we are deeply distressed and feel much pain over the present situation."

"Very sorry indeed, madame," Mrs. Jenkinson added, "we really did not intend for any of this to happen!"

"Silence!" she cried.

"Lady Catherine," I spoke up, "Charlotte and Mrs. Jenkinson have some vital information that it is best for us all to hear."

Lady Catherine's eyes shifted, then she rang the bell for her butler to come.

"Dalton," she informed him, "rather than have the tea set up and arranged in here, have it put in my study and have enough chairs brought in so that my guests can be properly accommodated there."

"Very good, ma'am," Dalton replied, and he left us again.

"We must talk of mundane things now," Lady Catherine demanded, "of common talk that you speak of when you return from somewhere." She turned to Charlotte and Mrs. Jenkinson. "I hope that you both had enough presence of mind to make sure this situation was treated delicately and not all the servants were informed."

"Yes," Mrs. Jenkinson responded, "I told Dalton, who only told your most trusted servants, so that they could pursue the… individuals. And those servants are sworn to silence."

"I remember reading about how masters in classic times would kill servants after they had them undergo covering up a secret," Lady Catherine recalled. "Barbaric tradition, but I do not deny that now I understand their logic."

We all raised our eyebrows and looked at each other. I looked at Charlotte, and we exchanged a glance of embarrassment.

"So," Lady Catherine said to Charlotte and Mrs. Jenkinson, "try and do the right thing of asking us how our journey was."

"How was your journey, madame?" Mrs. Jenkinson asked. "Were the roads dry?"

"Tolerable," Lady Catherine answered, "tolerable. Yet there were no broken wheels or carriages being overturned, therefore, that was all sufficient. Darcy and Mr. Bingley, you both spent most of the journey on horseback. I would not recommend doing such a thing in the future."

"An old habit," Mr. Darcy said. "Bingley and I are accustomed to riding alongside each other."

"Yes," Bingley piped up, "even when there is room enough in a carriage, we find freedom in riding on horseback. It is one of the pleasures of life."

"You speak that way now, but when your horse throws you one day, you will change your way of thinking," Lady Catherine commented. "Only travel on horseback when it cannot be helped, or for exercise, and that is all. The rest of the time, just ride in a carriage. You will do well to listen to my advice. In circumstances such as this, I am always right."

There are few absolutes in life, and Lady Catherine is one of them. To be sure, no county is fully complete without a great lady, in a grand home, who no matter what tragedy she is undergoing, she will always find the time to rule over others.

Dalton entered and told us that the tea was properly set up in Lady Catherine's study. We all went inside the safe confinements of the room, closing the door behind us. Once we were alone, Charlotte and Mrs. Jenkinson began to serve our tea for us, without even being asked first. It was evident that this was a part of their duties when they are at Rosings.

"Now that we are safe to talk about it," Lady Catherine said, "there is news."

"Yes," Mrs. Jenkinson said, then she turned to Charlotte. Typical! She did not want to be the one to tell Lady Catherine about the inevitable. Charlotte stepped forward with a letter in her hand.

"First," Charlotte said, "Dalton did send servants to try and reach Anne and Mr. Orwell, but by the time they reached the Blacksmith's shop, it was too late. They had too much of an advantage. The Blacksmith informed us that a priest had married them."

"Blacksmith shop?" Jane asked. "What part would a blacksmith shop play in this?"

"Gretna Green is the closest place to London that will marry people who are not twenty-one years old and don't have their parents' consent to marry," Elena explained. "And the first place that elopers get to when they reach Gretna Green is the Blacksmith Shop. In Gretna Green, you don't have to marry in a church. Because it is the first place that they reach, priests have been known to quickly be called on. You pay them a few shillings or guineas and they marry you in the smith shop. Often, it's said that when the smithy banged his gavel, it sounded out another set of elopers who finally wed."

"Married in a smith shop!" Lady Catherine cried. "My daughter really got married in a place where horseshoes are made?"

"Yes," Charlotte answered, barely higher than a whisper. "They must have worried that they were being pursued, so they didn't take the time to go to a church to do it. When Dalton sent the riders, they first stopped at the smithy, gave a description of Anne and Mr. Orwell, the blacksmith there confirmed that he banged his hammer when they married, and they had left a few hours before the riders arrived."

With each word spoken, Lady Catherine looked more dejected and despondent. Lydia leaned into Kitty and whispered.

"I had no idea that I would be married in a smithy shop. Thank goodness that I escaped that fate."

Lady Catherine shook her head. "My daughter married in the worst sort of way. Not only did she marry so utterly beneath her, but in the presence of a blacksmith. I can never forgive her. And we are really too late."

"We were always going to be, unfortunately," Colonel Fitzwilliam noted. "Aunt Catherine, by the time we left Brighton, the elopement would have already been successful. We are here to help you through this troubling time."

"And to safely see Anne returned home," Darcy added.

"She will never come home," Lady Catherine spat, "because I will not allow her to."

"Aunt Catherine…"

"I will not!"

Charlotte hesitated, but she then produced the letter again.

"This all can be confirmed by the letter that Anne sent us that arrived this morning."

Lady Catherine looked at the letter as if it was pandora's box.

"Well," Lady Catherine snapped, "I am not going to let that letter reach my hands, so read it if you will."

Charlotte began to read the letter.

Dear Charlotte & Mrs. Jenkinson,

I apologize for any discomfort that my actions will cause you. Please do not despise yourselves or take any blame for my actions. There was no manner for which you could have stopped me. Once it became evident that my mother was going to Brighton, I saw this as my chance to obtain liberty in the only manner that I saw fit. It is important for me to inform you both that I am now Mrs. Anne Orwell, and I have never been happier a day in my life. Mr. Orwell and I did not intend to fall in love, but we did, and I regard this as being the happiest of accidents.

With any good fortune, Mama will return to Rosings soon and she can hear this part of the letter.

Mother, I know that you must hold me in contempt now, and that you have spoken with heated words about my new husband. He is very aware that he must look like the worst of libertines. Therefore, I shall urge you now to believe that he only eloped at my behest. Faith, the scheme of running off to Gretna Green, was my idea. After we fell in love, I made a joke of doing so, but he would always dissuade me, hoping that God would give us the chance of your heart relenting, but I did not believe so. I knew that you would always regard him as being too far beneath us, and perhaps he is, but I do not care for that. He is kind to me, is considerate, has never shown himself to be vicious, and with him being a man of the cloth, I am certain that he shall feel the obligations to be kind to me.

I love you, Mother, and I never wish to cross you in this way, but I must be with the man that I love. I do not want to marry out of an arrangement that I didn't control. I am content that I have done right.

However, I know that your habit will lead to you not wishing to see me again for quite some time. My dear Mr. Orwell and I have decided to stay away from Rosings for a month, to give you time to recover from my elopement. Truly, Mama, I do not wish to cause you any pain, and I hope that you can forgive me, in time. And please believe that I write this of my own free will, and under no coercion on Mr. Orwell's part.

In a month, I shall write to you again, in hopes that you will receive us at Rosings and will welcome my new husband.

And please do not berate and blame Mrs. Collins and Mrs. Jenkinson, for they are blameless. The only way through which I was able to go through with the elopement was because you were absent from Rosings, giving me the opportunity to successfully persuade Mr. Orwell to the elopement. For, seeing this as the only chance for us to become one, he was more amenable to my plan.

I love you—please remember that.

Your loving daughter,
Anne

"I will never forgive her!" Lady Catherine cried, grabbing the letter, and throwing it in the fire.

We all watched as the letter burned in the fireplace, silenced under Lady Catherine's wrath.

"Aunt…" Colonel Fitzwilliam began.

"No, Richard! I will not forgive her."

"She is your only daughter."

"I don't have a daughter."

"But you do," Mr. Darcy urged. "And while we cannot undo what is done, we can do our best to safeguard Anne's future."

"And also secure Anne's present," I spoke up.

"What do you mean, Lizzy?" Georgiana asked me.

"Well," I deduced, "Charlotte, I am of the suspicion that Anne did not send an address on the letter."

"No, she didn't. She wrote her name on it, but no return address."

"I know that she says that she is writing that letter under her own free will, but we need to find her to make sure of that. I know that Mr. Orwell has given the impression of being a nice man, but history is full of wicked men appearing as being nice."

"You think that Mr. Orwell could be holding Anne against her will?" Charlotte asked.

"I doubt it, but we still have to make sure. Because what if I am wrong, and Anne eloped with him at first, but then she changed her mind, and he forced her hand, threatening her to write the letter to make it appear as if she is acting on her own volition."

"That is a happy thought," Lady Catherine declared, "for her to be doing everything against her own will, that would mean that she was forced into it."

"I do not think it probable," I urged her to believe, "I am only saying this to prepare for the worst scenario that could occur, and to help you understand that we should still look for her."

"But we do not know where to look," Mrs. Jenkinson extoled. "We have asked his servants of where their master could be. We did this under the guise of wondering where our clergyman was, but they didn't know."

I considered this.

"Even if Anne took money with her, they are staying away for a month," I theorized. "And sometimes, the only way for a couple to be away for so long, is if one of them is familiar with their surroundings. That is the only way to live somewhere without incurring any debts. Lady Catherine, does Anne know of any places in Scotland or in England that she is very familiar with?"

"I made sure that she was always safely at Rosings, or she travelled with me," Lady Catherine said.

"So, that means nowhere for her. But what of Mr. Orwell? Where is he from? Or what is he familiar with?"

"He received his education at Oxford," Lady Catherine said, "and he mentions that his uncle helped finance him for a time, but his uncle passed away a few years ago. His uncle owned a house but had no estate or wife. Therefore, Mr. Orwell received some money in an inheritance, but the house was sold on his uncle's passing."

"But where is Mr. Orwell from himself?" I asked again.

"Well, now that I think of it, he never mentioned it."

"You never asked?" Mr. Darcy questioned. "Aunt, that is not like you."

"Since he was raised, for a time, in Northampton, and went to Oxford, and his uncle died, I didn't need any more inquiries—especially since that was all that he spoke of."

"The parsonage!" I wondered. "At the parsonage, there must be some identification, a birth certificate, or letters perhaps from a correspondence that he has continued from his birthplace or something. Often, I've rarely heard of there being no trail of evidence anywhere."

"Ingenious," Mr. Darcy responded.

"How does your mind work, I wonder," Lady Catherine considered, critically.

"The way any woman's mind works when her father died and she had to grow up quickly," I responded. "I realized that I had no more moments to lose."

"Miss Elizabeth," Mr. Darcy responded, "would you be willing to ride side-saddle behind me? We need to go to Hunsford Parsonage."

"Yes, I can," I responded, standing up.

"I should go with you," Colonel Fitzwilliam said, standing up.

"Our aunt needs you to stay," Darcy advised. "Besides, I love you aunt, but Richard and Bingley, I need you both to ensure that my aunt doesn't mistreat my sisters and cousin."

"I am not going to cook them and eat them, Darcy," Lady Catherine declared.

"Aunt, I do not know that."

Together, we exited the house, Darcy ordered his horse, placed me on side-saddle behind him, and we rode off to the parsonage.

"How did you do it?" He roared over the wind as we rode.

"Do what?" I asked.

"Make such deductions."

"Honestly, I had no idea that I had an investigational side."

"Well, you do. You made me proud, Elizabeth."

"I love you."

"And I love you. Just make sure to continue having that investigational side when we have children. If you do, then they will never be able to get away with being troublemakers."

"Never fear. I saw how my parents raised Lydia, so I've had plenty of practice."

We reached the parsonage and the servants let us enter. Under the excuse of worrying about Mr. Orwell's whereabouts, Darcy requested that we be given entry to his study, where all his letters and other papers of import were stored. Knowing him to be Lady Catherine's aunt, as well as being very intimidated by Darcy, they accepted this eagerly, and we soon found ourselves running through Mr. Orwell's desks and other areas of the room.

"I love how intimidating you are, sometimes," I said, looking through Mr. Orwell's account book. "It really helps to get things moving."

"My demeaner has served me well over the years," he responded, looking through some more papers.

"I found something strange," I said, looking through his accounts.

"What?"

"Every month, Mr. Orwell sends precisely thirty pounds to another account. The only thing written to who it's sent to are initials: M.R. But it never corresponds to anything that has to do with the house or any expenses that Mr. Orwell would make for himself."

"Because it is not for himself," he replied.

"How could you know that?" I asked.

"Because of the letter that I just found. I think he was sending that money to his sister."

Abandoning the account book, I joined him at the desk, where he was holding a letter.

"He has a sister?"

"Her name is Marianne Rintoul. The drawer that I took it from is filled with their correspondence. Read this."

Leaning over his shoulder, I began.

My dearest Robert,

Once more, I thank you again for sending most of your inheritance to our household. Every month, your gift helps my family, which seems to be growing every year. I am keenly aware that not all men would be so generous for their sisters, let alone their half-sister who married for love. Thank you for encouraging me to follow my heart, because it has led to such happy ends. I always talk about you to your nieces and nephews, who wonder what their Uncle Robert is like. They know that you are a hero to us, and that we owe you much.

And truly, I am once more with child, and if all goes well, you will be an uncle for the sixth time. If my dear husband and I do not stop, I fear that we will have over ten children. To answer any worries that you wrote about in your last letter, you need never fear. Walter is still treating me very well and continues to be a different man than the man he was before we met. He still loves me, and I suffer no mistreatment at all. Brother, you grew into the perfect sort of clergyman, who understands that everyone deserves a second chance. I still do not want you to expose your connection to us, for your future is bright, and I fear that any connection to a sister who is married to an ex-convict will hinder your career. Still, do not mention us, because I do not want us to be the means through which your life is destroyed. You are a rare man of the cloth who understands forgiveness and tolerance. But the rest of the world is not so kind. Abandon all naivete that all are as good as you.

Be safe, brother, and remember that you save us all.

Your loving sister,

Marianne

When Mr. Darcy lowered the letter, it all became clear.

"Mr. Orwell didn't speak of his family, because his sister is married to a man who once was incriminated," I commented.

"And what was his crime?" Mr. Darcy asked. "This is frightening."

"With our criminal system," I observed, "it could have been a crime with no lasting effects. Some crimes are merely incidents that young men commit in the folly of their youth. We don't know the particulars yet. Still, Mr. Orwell was kind for sending his inheritance to his sister. Either way…" I looked on the back of the letter and saw that Marianne lived in—, "Edinburgh. Darcy,

Marianne and her husband live in Edinburgh. Isn't that 66 miles from Gretna Green?"

"Yes, it is," he observed. "At worst, they are not there, but his sister could give us information on where he might be. Or at best, that's where Mr. Orwell took Anne."

"He has shown himself to be considerate enough to pardon his brother-in-law's past, give them his blessing, and give his half-sister most of his own inheritance. And she tells her children about him. So what are the chances that a man who cares that much for his family would not be enticed to visit there and show off his new wife?"

"They really might be there."

"They really might be."

Mr. Darcy turned to me, and I read his look. Pulling me to him, he kissed me passionately again.

"Even if they are not there," he pointed out, "I marvel at your mind."

"Kiss me again."

"Right."

We kissed once more.

CHAPTER 7

THE ROAD STRETCHES AHEAD FOR US

On returning to the house, we told the family everything that we had discovered.

"It is the best option that we have to consider," Mr. Darcy finalized. "I propose that Richard and I travel to Edinburgh post-haste and see if our findings are correct."

"I am willing to leave immediately," Colonel Fitzwilliam said, but I was disturbed.

"Without me?" I asked. "I want to go with you."

"Miss Elizabeth," Lady Catherine countered, "chasing after elopers is not the actions of a lady."

"As you have pointed out on numerous occasions," I opposed, "I am not a lady in your eyes, so why should that matter now?"

"Elizabeth," Mr. Darcy asserted, "I believe that you ought to remain here."

I felt offended and betrayed, without being able to identify why that was.

"Why?" I snapped. "I have just as much a right to go as you do. Even though she is not my cousin, she will be one day."

"It is possibly dangerous."

"How? Does Anne plan to stick me with a fork?"

"Also, Richard and I are intending to depart in a matter of minutes and shall be traveling by horseback. It is faster."

"I presume that it is, but speed is of no use now," I argued, "because the most I can delay you all by traveling in a carriage is a day, and that won't change anything at all. If they are there when we arrive, they will still be married. Besides, if we travel by carriage, then you will not have to change horses at inns and overwork the poor beasts."

"Miss Bennet—" Colonel Fitzwilliam began.

"No!" I interrupted. "No other argument will do. And if you try and leave without me, I will stand in front of your horses and cause a spectacle."

"And this is the woman that you want to marry?" Lady Catherine said to Darcy.

"Aunt, you swore not to offend her," he said, "and Elizabeth does this out of consideration of being in my company. Besides, she is correct. Our going in a carriage will not change events."

"Then…" Kitty said, "can I go too?"

"This is getting outrageous," Lady Catherine bellowed. "This is a rescue to recover a captured woman, not a holiday."

"Two women going might make it easier if we do see Anne," Kitty added, "because by the men going, it looks like Anne is coming to be chastised and dragged back home. But if two women go as well, then Anne might let us confide in her more, because women are more open to speaking to other women about these sorts of things."

"Precisely," I added, "and if Anne is with these Rintouls, then having us women with the men would give the Rintouls a better impression."

"Despite my better judgment," Colonel Fitzwilliam admitted, "those are wise deductions."

"Kitty and Elizabeth," Darcy demanded, "be ready to go within ten minutes."

Taking Kitty's arm, I turned to Jane and Mr. Bingley.

"Make certain that neither gentlemen leave without us," I ordered.

"Yes," Jane confirmed.

Kitty and I rushed out of the library, went to our rooms where our bags were still packed, we grabbed one of them that we knew had a full change of clothes and rushed back downstairs just as

Colonel Fitzwilliam and Mr. Darcy were in the vestibule, with one piece of luggage each, waiting for the carriage to be brought round.

When I rushed up to them, I saw Mr. Darcy scowling at me. Pulling me aside he whispered his objections.

"Elizabeth, you have angered me," he began.

"I know," I said, "and I am sorry for it."

"In the future, if you ever disagree with me, you must do it in private. In the world we live in, a man cannot be seen always giving into his wife. It is not because I do not respect you, but because if you don't respect me, then no one will."

"Oh," I realized. "I had not thought of that. I just wanted to be with you."

"I know, but in the future, we must be unified in public. That is the only way that I will both look and stay strong." He patted my cheek. "Promise me, my love."

"I promise."

"I am happy that you are coming."

"Besides," I said. "I have another plan."

"Another one?" he asked, his eyes narrow. "Where do you come up with these plans?"

"I do not know. They just come to me."

Everyone saw us off to the carriage, and Mr. Bingley was the last one to speak to us before we closed the door.

"Be safe," Mr. Bingley advised, "and make certain to take every opportunity to look after yourselves properly."

"We will," Darcy responded, "remember to look after my family, Bingley."

"I will."

Colonel Fitzwilliam looked past Bingley and at Jane, who was behind him.

"Sometimes," Colonel Fitzwilliam confessed freely, "I wonder how you and I can stand the sight of each other."

"I wonder that often myself," Mr. Bingley considered, "but we do it very well."

"Yes, we do."

The carriages took off, and we were once more on the road.

"It feels like we just arrived," Kitty observed. "Oh but wait. We did."

We chuckled at this as Rosings disappeared behind us.

"Neither Darcy nor I will take it amiss if either of you fall asleep," Colonel Fitzwilliam encouraged. "You earned it."

"I had a plan to tell you, but it can wait," I said, closing my eyes.

"You did?" Colonel Fitzwilliam questioned. "Where do you come up with these plans?"

"I asked her the same thing," Mr. Darcy pointed out. "It is better to just let her have her mysteries."

Kitty followed suit and also closed her eyes. Half-awake, I saw her head roll to the side and Colonel Fitzwilliam let her head rest on his shoulder. He even leaned more toward her so that her head could rest more gently against him.

"How did it come to this?" I heard Darcy ask his cousin. "How did our lives take this turn?"

"The side-effects to being born to wealth," Colonel Fitzwilliam answered. "Our good fortune must be repaid for by a little bit of scandal and discomfort along the way. No one can have everything."

At last, I gave in and fell asleep.

A few hours later, I woke up to find that we had arrived in London, where we broke our journey at a hotel to rest and help the horses replenish themselves.

The next day, we set off very early, arrived at Gretna Green in a few of hours, and proceeded onward to Edinburgh. Every now and again, we stopped to give our horses some rest, then we continued on, reaching the city in a few days. We stopped at an inn, where we were seen to immediately, due to our appearance of affluence, and we sat down to dinner in Darcy's and Richard's room.

"I've asked the hotel owner about the address on Mrs. Rintoul's letter," Colonel Fitzwilliam said, "and he said that he can lend us one of his coachmen from his stables. The man's name is Garvie. He will take us to the address tomorrow."

"Very good," Kitty said. "Hopefully, this journey was not for nothing. Now, Elizabeth, are you ready to tell us your plan?"

"Yes," I said. "I've enough time to think it over, and I do believe it is worth trying. When I consider Mrs. Rintoul's letter to her brother, Mr. Orwell does appear to be a good man. But we still cannot fully rule out the prospect that he is still a fortune hunter. For yes, he does care about his family, but he could be using Anne to help them. For their sake, this is good, but for Anne's sake, she should not be married off just to relieve the suffering of Mr. Orwell's relations. Therefore, just in case we are wrong, and he did not marry her out of love, we have to test him."

"You are thinking of Anne's dowry, aren't you?" Darcy asked me.

"Yes. What if Mr. Orwell was of the belief that Anne's dowry was left to her 'in condition' only, and that her mother is willing to shift all the estate to you or the Colonel? By doing so, we can truly see what Mr. Orwell's love is worth?"

"And if it proves to be a false love," Colonel Fitzwilliam said, "I cannot bear the idea of Anne living with the runaway clergyman, but I also fear the idea of her annulling the marriage."

"As long as the marriage is annulled privately," Darcy considered, "then what could be the harm?"

"In a public way, nothing at all, but in a private way that can have negative effects on Anne's mind."

"Perhaps so," Kitty said. "I have never met Anne, so I would not know how she would react to this sort of situation. But we women often die of broken hearts on the stage or in poetry, but not in real life. We have our cry out, let it rest in our minds for a few months, and then we do recover. We'd have to hope that your cousin is similar. But, if my opinion is worth anything, it would be better to check Mr. Orwell's intentions, and if they did prove mercenary, then we ought to remove your cousin from him, in the most permanent way that there is."

Colonel Fitzwilliam turned to Darcy.

"Our women have spoken."

"Yes," Darcy confirmed, "yes, they have."

The next morning came, we ordered an early breakfast and arranged for Garvie to prepare to lead us to Mrs. Rintoul's address. He was awake and on time, and we rode out to the outskirts of Edinburgh. The houses were less affluent and more modest, but it was nothing that we had not seen before with the farmers in Hertfordshire. Our carriage made all the occupants on the street turn and gaze, wondering what sort of individuals would wish to come there, and we arrived at the address.

"This is the house?" Mr. Darcy asked Garvie.

"This is the address, sir," Garvie responded. "I know this area well. I was raised here."

"Sorry to have doubted you."

"The house does not look rundown or ill-taken care of," I noted to Darcy. "It appears to be clear and well looked after. It's a workman's house."

"But what of the people inside?" Darcy questioned. "That is the real crisis."

We walked up to the door and Darcy knocked on it. Very soon, a young boy, around the age of twelve, opened it. He was dressed modestly, but properly, and his face was clean.

"Good day," he asked us.

"Good day," we replied, uncertain.

"And who might you all be?" he asked. "Forgive me, but I cannot allow anyone inside who has not told me their names."

"Oh, you are quite the precocious boy," I remarked.

"I do not know what that word means."

"It means that you act very maturely for your age."

He grinned at that. "Oh, thank you."

"I am Mr. Fitzwilliam Darcy of Pemberley," Darcy said, removing his hat. "This is my cousin, Colonel Fitzwilliam, the younger son of the Earl of Matlock, and this is Miss Elizabeth Bennet, and Miss Kitty Bennet, of Longbourn. Is this the Rintouls home?"

"Yes, it is. My father is at work, but my mother is home."

"We would like to speak to her," Colonel Fitzwilliam said, "but we were wondering if you have seen any two individuals. One of them is our cousin. Her name is Anne."

"You are Aunt Anne's cousins?" he asked, his eyes beaming. "You came to see us, too?"

We all looked at each other. Now it was all confirmed.

"Yes," I said, "we have."

"Mama!" the boy cried, "Anne's cousins are here to visit us." He looked back at us. "I am Vincent."

"Nice to make your acquaintance, Vincent," Kitty responded.

"You may come in," Vincent said, inviting us into the parlor. We all obeyed, and he looked at Colonel Fitzwilliam. "You are a colonel, sir?"

"I am."

"When I get older and I get my mother's permission, I plan to enlist."

"That is very good," Colonel Fitzwilliam encouraged. "His majesty's army could do with some strong lads like yourself."

Vincent grinned again as his mother entered, with a baby in her arms.

"Oh," she commented, overwhelmed when seeing us all there, with Darcy and the Colonel looking so imposingly handsome and of a higher class than she was used to entertaining. "My goodness. Good day to you all."

"Good morning," Darcy replied, then he introduced us all and explained his connection. "Colonel Fitzwilliam and I are Anne de Bourgh's cousins, and we came to inquire after her. We understand that she is here, visiting you all, since you are her new family."

"That is very much so," she responded, handing her baby to Vincent. "Vincent, take Olivia upstairs and look after her."

"Yes, Mama," Vincent replied, taking his little sister and carrying her upstairs.

"You have a fine boy," Colonel Fitzwilliam observed.

"Thank you," Mrs. Rintoul said. "His father is not present because he is a chimney sweep. Between his efforts, and the kind efforts of my brother always being so generous with his money, I am able to keep my children well looked after." She looked away from us, making sure that she could not be overheard. "I know why you are here. I know that my brother eloped with your cousin. And I am to guess that you have come to retrieve her."

Her sudden attack on the subject disconcerted us, but I was happy that she had done so. This gave us the ability to get to the point.

"So, you know everything?" Mr. Darcy asked.

"My brother told me soon after they arrived. He sent a letter first, to prepare us for their coming. The day after they stayed, he told me the truth of the matter."

"So, they are living here?" Mr. Darcy looked around us all, at the extreme simplicity of the house.

"Yes, they are. Tell me the truth. Are you coming to take her back?"

"We have come because our cousin ran off with a clergyman who has now made a mockery of his profession and they eloped. Perhaps, maybe, we did come to retrieve her."

"First," she said, "I will not have you slander my brother at all in this house. Regardless of what you think, he is a good man."

"But we do not know that," Colonel Fitzwilliam responded. "Forgive us for our bluntness, but all that we know is that our aunt's reverend ran off with her daughter while she was away. And that woman is an heiress to a large estate. You must understand that we have no choice but to come here, very much dubious of your brother's actions."

"I understand that, however, it is my duty to defend him. You could not see or imagine how much he has done for me and my family over the years. He is a good man and would not run off with a woman unless he was attached to her. Being mercenary is not his way."

"Is he and our cousin here, at present?"

"No, they have taken a walk to the church. That was perhaps an hour ago, and so we expect them here any minute. Until then, could I offer you all some coffee?"

"Yes," I said, "that would be lovely."

She left the room, and we all were left to debate all that had occurred.

"It's hard seeing the sister of the man who I wished to throttle," Darcy observed. "It now makes everything more complicated."

"We told you," Kitty observed, "the effect of a lady being present."

"But what puzzles me are the living conditions," Colonel Fitzwilliam continued. "Anne really is staying here?"

"That is what puzzles me," Darcy added. "She is used to being waited on, in a luxurious home with lots of servants. How could she be happy here?"

"Perhaps she is not," I observed, "and merely puts up with it for Mr. Orwell's sake."

Mrs. Rintoul entered again, with a tray of cups and coffee.

"I can help you," Kitty offered, helping her pour and prepare the coffee for us all.

As we all sat there, drinking, I thought it best to keep the conversation on family.

"So, you have six children?" I asked.

"Yes. Each time we think we are done, but then another one comes forth. I never knew that I had the ability to love so many children. But we all become accustomed to it. Vincent is the eldest, then there is Thomasina, Josephine, Clarence, Hector, and Olivia at the end."

"Where are your other children?" I asked.

"They are at a neighbor's house, playing with their children. Poor Vincent has reached that age where he has finished school and is no longer interested in playing with toys. He is growing serious. It is the hardest thing in the world to watch your children no longer wish to remain as children. That is the real pain of it. Do any of you have children yourselves?"

"Not yet," Mr. Darcy responded, "but I hope to on the completion of our marriage," he said, gesturing to me.

"We are engaged," I explained.

"Ah," she said, "the most romantic time to be. I love my

children, but there is no way to describe the moments before, when it was just you and your husband."

"These times do feel like the passionate eclipse," I agreed. "I wish it would last."

"In many ways, it does. My husband and I still love each other. I hope that your fortune is the same." Next, she looked at Colonel Fitzwilliam and Kitty.

"Oh," Kitty corrected, "he and I are merely their family, and we came along to express our support of the others."

"Yes," Colonel Fitzwilliam corrected. "That is all."

"You care for your family," Mrs. Rintoul observed. "I know the joys of that."

"Mrs. Rintoul," I asked, "I do not mean to sound indelicate, but I must ask. I am merely obligated to. Your husband, Mr. Rintoul. From my understanding, he has a criminal history."

"You must please hear me explain what happened before you judge my husband."

"We are anxious to hear the truth."

"My husband's crime was a crime of necessity and had no malicious intent behind it at all. He was arrested and imprisoned because he was a thief."

"A thief?" Kitty repeated.

"A thief due to hunger," she continued. "Before we met, my husband was very poor, could not find work, and he was often starving. One time, he stumbled on a bakery, so he broke the window and stole some food from there. He was eventually caught and sentenced to two years in prison."

"Two years?" I gasped. "That much?"

"Not all courts have compassion in them," she continued, "but he was lucky while in prison. He befriended a man who knew how to get them both work when they were released. Once he was, he began work as a chimney sweep, and has been doing such ever since. We met a couple months after his release."

"And in all that time," Colonel Fitzwilliam asked, "has your husband ever given you cause for alarm?"

"Never. First, his crime was out of desperation for survival, and not malicious intent. Also, when a man is punished so severely, they don't wish to undergo that punishment again. So, they spend their lives making up for it. If the result of getting a saint for a husband was that he was initially a sinner, then I am more than happy with that circumstance."

We heard voices outside. Anne de Bourgh was about to face us.

CHAPTER 8

A GOOD HEART

The door opened and a man entered with Miss Anne de Bourgh beside him. She had been laughing merrily, her face alight in a manner that I had never seen before.

"Marianne, we are returned—" he was cut off when he saw us. Anne's spirit deflated immediately when seeing her cousins and me, and her face looked horror-stricken, losing all its happiness. In that moment, I didn't care at all if they had eloped. I could tell that he brought her a happiness that she perhaps had never known before.

"Good morning, Anne," Mr. Darcy said, standing up alongside Colonel Fitzwilliam.

"Cousin," Colonel Fitzwilliam added.

"Fitzwilliam and Richard," Anne said, holding onto Mr. Orwell's arm. "I had not thought that Mama would send you."

Mr. Orwell placed his body in front of Anne, protectively.

"Sister?" Mr. Orwell asked Mrs. Rintoul.

"Vincent had them enter before I knew they were here," Mrs. Rintoul responded. "When I came downstairs, there was no way that I could tell them to leave. Robert, I am sorry."

"It is not her fault," Colonel Fitzwilliam said. "As family to Anne, we have every right to discover where our cousin was."

Anne looked past her cousins and at Kitty and me.

"Good morning, Mrs. Orwell," I greeted her, "this is my sister,

Miss Kitty Bennet. Kitty, this is Mrs. Anne Orwell, Lady Catherine de Bourgh's daughter."

"A pleasure to make your acquaintance, Mrs. Orwell," Kitty said. "I offer you my congratulations."

"Thank you," Anne said, hopeful. "It is a pleasure to meet you again, Miss Bennet, and to make your acquaintance, Miss Kitty." Then she looked at her cousins. "Please, hear us out before you judge us. Fitzwilliam and Richard, please, do not take me away from my husband. Besides, you cannot now, because we are married, and it is legal."

"Anne," Colonel Fitzwilliam urged, "do you know the pain you have caused your mother by this elopement?"

"I feel sorry for her distress, and I did not mean to cause her any alarm," Anne said, "but I had to. You all know that Mama would have never encouraged the match. I acted out of desperation, but not out of lack of consideration. Also, please do not berate my husband, for this was my idea."

"An idea that I was eager to accept," Mr. Orwell responded. "Mr. Darcy and Colonel Fitzwilliam, I have heard much of you both. I imagine that you never heard of me till recently."

"That is so," Mr. Darcy responded, "your name was one that never was brought forward in one moment to the next."

"Darcy," I whispered, reprimanding him gently, while taking his hand. "You must understand, Mr. Orwell, that Mr. Darcy is merely being protective of his cousin."

"I understand that," Mr. Orwell said, "but I beg of you to direct any negative words at me, and not at Anne. She only committed to this rash action because she knew that it was the only way to be together. I take full responsibility on myself for our elopement, but I do not regret what I have done or what I have failed not to do. Please believe that I do love Anne."

"How do we know that?" Darcy asked. "How do we know that you are not marrying her for her money?"

"That does me a great injustice, sir, but I understand that you ask that of me. Anne and I have fallen in love, and there was no chance of us being happy with anyone else."

"Please believe him," Anne said. "He speaks truly. Besides,

Fitzwilliam, surely you don't want what my mother asks of us. You didn't want us to marry any more than I."

"That is true," Darcy confirmed. "You have saved us both in that manner. But I wish that it had been achieved in a different way."

"Then we will see his love being put to the test," Colonel Fitzwilliam said. "Mr. Orwell, if you have the courage to run off with our cousin, then you will accept us to ask you to consider what that means. We speak for her mother, and we will tell you what your actions have led to, if you will speak with us alone."

"No!" Anne gasped.

"Mrs. Orwell," I assured her, "surely you know that your cousins have no malicious intent. They just wish to speak to your new husband, so that he understands what happens if he shall stay married to you. They will just be informing him of a truth that your mother has told us about your finances."

"My finances?" Anne repeated. "I am an heiress."

"That may change," Mr. Darcy confirmed, then he turned to Mr. Orwell. "Sir, we humbly ask you to hear us out, consider what we have to tell you, and then consult with Anne afterwards. If we are to be family, then we have this right to ask you."

"Marianne," Mr. Orwell said to his sister, "make sure that Anne is treated well."

"Yes, brother," Mrs. Rintoul assured him. Mr. Orwell stepped forward, straightening his waistcoat. "Gentlemen, if you would but join me in my brother-in-law's personal study."

The gentlemen left the room, leaving us women to confer alone.

———

"I have some biscuits," Mrs. Rintoul offered, "if any of you would like some."

We thanked her but assured her that the coffee was all that we needed.

"First," I said, "if you are happy, then that is something that I wished for you."

"I am happy," Anne pressed. "I don't care what anyone thinks, I am very happy. Aren't I, Mrs. Rintoul? Tell them. I have been smiling since I came."

"She has," Mrs. Rintoul confirmed, "despite that we are so much lower than she is, we have done our best to make her feel at home."

"I don't care about if anyone is lower or higher than me," Anne pressed. "I just want to be free from all of that. And I am. However temporary it may last here. And I don't understand, what are the men talking about?"

"It is a new development," Kitty answered, "where your mother has considered changing your inheritance."

"She has considered to give all her estate and fortune to your cousins, Mr. Darcy and her brother's sons, the Fitzwilliams," I said. "Anne, I do not like to tell you this, but she might give you nothing."

"She would not do that," Anne denied. "She may take much away from me, but surely, she wouldn't give me nothing. That is not like Mama to do that sort of thing."

"She might not, in the end," I said, instantly feeling terrible for my lie, but it had to be done. "But this is important for Mr. Orwell to consider."

Anne studied us.

"You don't think he would leave me once he realizes that I am penniless? No, Robert wouldn't do that."

"No indeed," Mrs. Rintoul agreed, "he would not!"

"Mr. Orwell is fortunate," I gathered, "to have you both believe in him to such a degree. I believe that you both are correct. Now we just have to wait for him to prove it."

Kitty addressed them both.

"Nothing else can be helped, so let us talk about pleasanter things. Mrs. Orwell and Mrs. Rintoul, how has it been when you both discovered that you both were now sisters?" she asked, "and how does married life suit you, Mrs. Orwell?"

Anne and Mrs. Rintoul began to tell us about this happy situation until the gentlemen returned to us. When they appeared, Mr. Orwell looked heavier.

"Robert?" Anne asked, standing up, worried about Mr. Orwell's grave expression. When seeing him, she was silenced, and her face dropped somewhat. He walked up to her and took her hands in his. "Robert," she repeated, her voice hollow and desperate. "What have they told you?"

"That I brought bad fortune on you when I married you," Mr. Orwell determined. "Anne, I am sorry."

"Sorry?" she repeated, her eyes about to tear up.

"And what I am about to ask of you is hard," he continued. "If your love for me is that strong, then I hope you will understand my asking it. Please hear me first before you judge. And if you feel that you cannot live without your fortune and large home, then I shall allow you to annul our marriage and I will rip up the marriage certificate. It will be your choice, Anne."

Holding their hands, they sat down together.

"Anne," he continued, "it has come to my attention that your mother shall sever all your inheritance and you shall be left with nothing if we choose to stay married. However, please consider, that if we can convince your family to keep our elopement a secret, then perhaps I can find another parish somewhere else, and I will fight to support us. If we economize, I can make sure that you have a couple of servants to tend to everything. I will do everything I can to provide for you and whatever family we may have. Look around you. This is perhaps the life that you shall have from thenceforth. If you could see yourself in this life, which I wish that you could, then you will make me very happy. But if you cannot suffer this life, then I will release you. Anne, I just want you to be happy."

It was a beautiful plea, delivered very well. In that moment, it was evident to us all that Mr. Orwell really did love Anne, and she did love him. It merely had been two people who had fallen in love from two different social spheres.

Taking his face in her hands, Anne kissed him passionately. We all looked away, out of modesty, and waited for their display of affection to end.

"My house was too large for me anyway," Anne said. "I hate the knowledge that one day, I had to look after it all. I despised that I had to marry for the sake of maintaining a level in society that I did not know how to live up to. I always was falling apart under the weight of such grandeur. If you can suffer a wife who is so useless that she brings you no money, then I can easily walk through life with you behind me."

"You will stay with me?" he realized, his face light from happiness again.

"Yes," she cried, "I will stay."

"God forgive me," he cried, holding her close to him. "Let no one tear us away from each other again. No, we will not be parted from each other, no!" Keeping her hands in his, Mr. Orwell turned to Mr. Darcy and Colonel Fitzwilliam. "I wish to believe that you both have some influence over your aunt. Can you please urge her to keep our elopement secret so that I can get work somewhere else, to look after her daughter? Also, if she would be so kind as to send Anne's belongings to our home when we find a parsonage, that would be perfect. At least Anne's treasured objects would be there to offer her comfort for anything else she has lost by marrying me."

"There is more hope than that," Mr. Darcy stated. "Lady Catherine never fully entertained severing all ties between Anne and her inheritance."

"What?" Anne said.

"In truth, we do not fully know the depths of her anger," Colonel Fitzwilliam supported, "but Miss Elizabeth knew that we needed to make sure that Mr. Orwell loved you."

"If a man still wants to marry a woman, despite that she is virtually penniless," I surmised, "then he really must be in love. Mr. Orwell, forgive me, but I had to make certain that your actions were not mercenary."

"I understand," Mr. Orwell said, "but does that mean that Anne has not lost anything by marrying me?"

"We cannot say for certain," Darcy acknowledged, "because Lady Catherine has not mentioned this. All that we ask is that you both come with us back to Kent. Face your mother, and then we will see where her mind has fallen on."

Anne closed her eyes, frustrated.

"She will hate me. I cannot bear the sight of it."

"I understand," Kitty remarked, "but that is something that you have to face sometime. It is best for you to face it now."

Anne looked at us both.

"Why have you both come?" she asked. "Miss Elizabeth, I know that I must mean so very little to you. Why have you both come to help me?"

"Because we will be family soon," I answered. "I am engaged to your cousin, Mr. Darcy."

Anne looked between us, smiling again.

"If so, then that will make it easier that I thwarted Mama's plans," she realized, "because you are engaged to each other, then she had no chance of being obeyed. My actions never would have mattered, because you already chose another, Fitzwilliam. I hope you both will be very happy, as I am."

"I believe we shall be," I said, "and you are stronger than I thought you ever were."

"I was given a chance. And for the longest time, I thought any chance of me being happy had ended."

"Well," Mr. Orwell said, aglow from knowing that Anne was staying with him, "Sister, if I were to buy some food at the market, do you think we can make a worthy dinner for my beloved's family for tonight?"

"I think so," Mrs. Rintoul confirmed, "if you go soon."

"We can depart for Rosings tomorrow morning," Mr. Orwell said, "but for today, allow us one more day of peace and let us invite you all to dinner."

"You are family now," Colonel Fitzwilliam said, "we happily accept."

We offered to escort Anne and Mr. Orwell to the grocers' shops, so that we could give Mrs. Rintoul time away from us. As we walked, we paired off, with Anne and Mr. Orwell in the front, Kitty and Colonel Fitzwilliam in the back, and Mr. Darcy and I in the middle.

"Well," I said, "there is naturally no written script for how to react to seeing two people who eloped, but I do believe that this could not have gone better, given the circumstances."

"In the end, we might have been fortunate," Darcy said. "This is the happiest that I have ever seen Anne. She had a glow to her now."

"She is a woman in love. And he loves her. She has succeeded where many have not had the chance: she met someone who loves her in return. Life is full of those who go unloved by the ones that they loved. She has not had that pain."

"And when all things are considered, perhaps this was the best match for her. Mr. Orwell does seem like a steady man who is kind. She needs kindness and steadiness. In truth, she lived in Rosings Park, but she never became a part of it. I suppose that she never really had the chance."

"The question now becomes... what else does life have in store for them?"

Due to so many children being at the house, the dinner was very comfortable to sit through and the food was well-prepared. For when there are six children in a house, there is no chance of uncomfortable silences.

At last, we met Mr. Rintoul. He was a large and strong man, who clearly was an imposing figure who had a soft and gentle expression. He proved to be an entertaining man, and it was very evident that he did love his wife very much. With a man who understood how to properly display affection, a woman could not help but eventually feel flattered by such attentions. Mrs. Rintoul had no choice but to marry her husband, despite his background, because he was the sort of man who was worth marrying.

Mr. Orwell's comfort with his half-sister was very touching. For indeed, not everyone feels such depth for half-relations. I felt sorry for him. To be a clergyman who had to resort to eloping, was a painful thing. Although, he really had no choice in the matter.

The next day, it was time to depart. Anne and Mr. Orwell had their own carriage, and they rode in front of ours as we journeyed back to Kent. Our coachman was happy to return, for that had been the longest that he had been away from Rosings in years.

"I prefer leaving places that I'm not used to," he grunted, "I don't know where the dangers are. The sooner we get back to Kent, the better."

The Rintouls gave us a warm farewell and we set out, hoping to arrive in London as soon as we were able.

As we rode along, Kitty was looking uncertain.

"I know that look," I analyzed. "What is it for?"

"It is something that I have been meaning to ask," Kitty said, "and I was waiting for the right time. We have been facing many obstacles, and I knew that it was not right to ask something of anyone with all the woes added to our lives. But now that things are looking better, I feel that I can make my plea. Mr. Darcy, I have a favor to ask you. Please, hear me out first and understand that this favor will not cost you a pence, or even take any exertion on your part."

"What sort of favor asks so little?" he asked.

"Mr. Darcy, I am aware that you were not excited by me wishing to be a writer. I know that this was no easy prejudice for you. We women are not well-regarded in some circles for writing. However, there are women writers out there now, and after my reading at the ball in Brighton, I hope that was there to show you that the world is changing. In some ways. But it is remaining the same in others. When writing novels, it is more likely that you can get published if you are a man from a noteworthy family."

"Kitty," he realized, "are you asking me to borrow my name?"

"Only for a brief duration," Kitty rushed out, nervous. "Would you mind, if when I submit my book to publishers, that I write my name as Mr. K. M. Darcy, of the Darcy family. If I get anyone interested, I will enlighten them of the truth and then publish under the pseudonym 'a Lady'. If you feel that my deception is underhanded, actually, it is common. Many female writers have taken on male names when submitting their work, and then reveal themselves as women afterwards. The name Darcy will never appear on any book at all. It is just to help publishers take me seriously and consider me. Could you find this to be an agreeable arrangement?"

Mr. Darcy was silent for a moment, and it was intimidating.

"I cannot promise you that it will work," he said at last, "but I understand that this is the best way for you to become known. You may if you promise me one thing."

"Yes?"

"If publishers still do not want your book, then do not be disheartened. Novels are a very competitive industry."

"I understand that it may take me years," Kitty said, "or never. But I must try. Thank you, Mr. Darcy! You might have been my biggest hope. This means the world to me!"

Mr. Darcy smiled.

"I bid you good luck."

"I'll need it."

"Are you still planning on writing that romance about the soldier?" Colonel Fitzwilliam asked.

"I've already completed the first four chapters." She gave him a sideways glance. "Sorry, Colonel, but nothing you say will stop me."

"I had no wish to," he said, settling back with a smile.

CHAPTER 9

FACING THE FAMILY

At last, Anne de Bourgh found herself at Rosings Park. When we approached the houses and stepped down from our carriages, Anne looked as if she were heading for her doom.

"Courage, my love," Mr. Orwell encouraged, holding her hand. "This will be hard, but I do believe that this is a trial that must be faced."

"I feel as if all the labors in the bible would be easier to face than this."

"I can understand your fears but remember that we stand together."

Dalton exited, followed by the rest of our family—except for Lady Catherine. Jane, Mr. Bingley, Charlotte Collins, and Mrs. Jenkinson all greeted us warmly, and Anne felt happy that Charlotte and Mrs. Jenkinson were so warmhearted about it.

"I didn't mean to cause you distress," Anne assured them, "but I did what was necessary." Turning to Mr. Orwell, they linked arms. "I hope Mama was not severe upon you. If she was, I will make sure that she does not cast any blame on you both. But there! Have I not found a worthy husband?"

"Unfortunately, my worthiness is nothing compared to the wife that I have obtained," Mr. Orwell added. "I hope that you both shall one day believe the deep affection that I have for your mistress."

"I shall believe it," Charlotte responded, "provided that you always treat your new wife like the queen that she is."

"I can assure you that I always shall."

After introductions were made, it was apparent that Lady Catherine had not presented herself.

"Your mama is waiting for you in the main drawing room," Mrs. Jenkinson informed the new couple.

Anne drew in a deep sigh. "Yes."

We all entered, removed our cloaks and bonnets, and Dalton addressed us.

"Lady Catherine has expressly requested to see Mr. Orwell and her daughter alone."

We all looked at each other, and I leaned into Mr. Darcy, for he and I were at the back of the group, unable to be overheard.

"I fear that your aunt might intimidate them," I whispered. "Is there any way that you can go with them, to tell Lady Catherine about Mr. Orwell's steadfastness?"

"Yes, I had a mind to."

Mr. Darcy stepped forward and addressed the butler.

"I understand, Dalton, but please inform Aunt Catherine that Richard and I must press our company, to inform her of all that we witnessed. We cannot brook refusal right now, for the sake of giving her all the information that she deserves."

"Very good, sirs."

Colonel Fitzwilliam and Mr. Darcy joined Anne and Mr. Orwell as they went to meet the imposing Lady.

Left to our own devices, Charlotte took over. She arranged for tea and refreshments to be brought, our luggage to be taken back to our rooms, and when we were all seated in the summer breakfast room that Mr. Collins once compared to my Aunt Philip's parlor, we were at last alone and say to them all that had occurred.

"Was your journey without any impediment?" Jane asked.

"How were they when you found them?" Charlotte questioned.

"Is it true that they married in a blacksmith shop?" Elena inquired.

"And they look happy," Mrs. Jenkinson observed. "I want to

believe that Mr. Orwell is not a fortune hunter. It would help if you set my mind at rest about it."

"We can," Kitty confirmed. "Elizabeth had a plan of how to discover if Mr. Orwell had feet made of clay, and it turned out that Mr. Orwell proved himself to be a solid and sturdy man. Elizabeth, I do believe we have the right to tell them everything, especially since it has ended very well—so far."

"I do believe you are right." I gave in, looking at everyone who was around us. "For Mr. and Mrs. Orwell's sake, you ought to know the truth, so that you will think better of both of them."

I took another sip of tea and then Kitty and I told them everything since we had discovered them at Mr. and Mrs. Rintoul's home.

When we finished narrating it all, Georgiana placed her hand on her chest.

"While it is unconventional," Georgiana professed. "I cannot deny that it is romantic and that maybe this might be the best thing for Anne."

"I do believe that it might be," I added. "You all were not there. Anne truly looked happy when she was there. I never saw her look so exquisite. Her cheeks were red from having life in them and her eyes had light."

"It was always that way with Anne when she was in Mr. Orwell's company," Charlotte informed us. "They always were happy."

"That is why I was not too alarmed when I had learned of it," Mrs. Jenkinson said. "I only feared how Lady Catherine would take the news. Though, God forgive me, I do admit that I am very terrified now."

"Why so?" Mr. Bingley asked.

"Because somewhere within us all is a very selfish being. I am no different from anyone else. What I refer to is that now that Miss de Bourgh is married, what shall I do?"

"Oh, I don't know," I offered, "Lady Catherine does enjoy

having someone to advise and order the life of. Now that Anne is married, I do believe that she will still need company, and will want someone to tend to Anne. I don't believe that you will see the end of Rosings Park for a very long time."

"I hope you are correct, Lizzy," Charlotte professed, "for both our sakes."

Despite all the reassurance that was received with seeing Anne returned to Rosings, Lydia was the only one who didn't say anything. Indeed, she looked depressed throughout the whole conversation.

"And how are you, Lydia?" I asked when the conversation ended and there was an abrupt pause.

"I am well," she responded, having no energy behind her voice.

"You have not spoken a word since we arrived."

"Because I am so dejected," she responded, more heatedly, "about the hypocrisy that surrounds all of this. This Miss de Bourgh runs off and elopes, and you all are happy. I plan to do something similar, and you all chastise me for it! I do not think it fair. I do not think it's fair at all!"

She stood abruptly and dashed from the room, closing the door behind her. Without a moment to delay, Kitty stood up.

"I shall go after her, to make sure that she does no harm."

With that, Kitty left the room as well.

It was awkward. There was no way to cover the fact that it was awkward. Therefore, there was nothing left to do but confront the matter.

"Welcome to our family," I said.

Everyone laughed.

Thank goodness for empathic people!

A couple hours later, it was time for dinner. Dalton retrieved us all, and we entered the dining room to find Mr. Darcy, Colonel Fitzwilliam, the Orwells and Lady Catherine already there.

"Our main dish shall be seafood this evening," she explained, "and I shall inform you all of where you are seated." After telling us all who sat next to who, we began to eat, and it was as if nothing had happened!

Lady Catherine began to tell us all that we had missed while being away, from the little to the mundane. After mentioning how a neighbor of theirs had twin daughters that she had advised on what governess would be proper for them to send for, she elaborated on every detail. As is the way with Lady Catherine, she often spoke, but seldom needed anyone to answer. When that topic had been exhausted, she turned to us Bennet sisters.

"So," she observed, "I do believe that I have four of the five Bennet sisters here at Rosings Park."

"You do, your ladyship," I said.

"And the only one missing is which sister?"

"Mary, ma'am," Jane listed, "she is the third eldest."

"And if I got this right, you are the eldest, Miss Bennet, then Miss Elizabeth is next, making Miss Mary the third, Miss Kitty the fourth, and Miss Lydia is the fifth."

"Yes, I am the youngest," Lydia said boldly, "but all have the same experiences. We do much together."

"You were invited to Brighton, if I recall what you told me."

"Yes, I was."

"But by yourself, only to be companion to the Colonel's wife. Indeed, I do wonder what your mother was about! A young lady in a bathing-place without her mother to monitor her can get into all sorts of mischief."

Lydia looked down and continued to eat.

"If I had known your mother, I would have advised to go with you, bringing Miss Mary along as well. After all, it is already improper that your eldest sister was at home while you were away."

"Why so?" Lydia asked.

"Because you are the youngest, my dear. Miss Elizabeth already informed me that the youngest of you were out before the eldest were married. Miss Elizabeth believed that it was unfair for the youngest to be not out just because the eldest did not have the means or inclination to marry early. You did say that, Miss Elizabeth?"

"I did indeed," I affirmed. "Yes, sometimes a young lady is full young to be out in company. Yet I still believe that it would hardly encourage sisterly affection."

"I know that you believe so, but I stand firm with my assessment that it is best to not allow the youngest to be so up and about everything while the eldest are not settled. For, going against that has led to the eldest being at home, while the youngest was invited somewhere. It is not the way it should be. But do all you Bennet sisters believe in the same thing?"

"Well," Jane added, "as the eldest, I do not wish for my sisters to be deprived of opportunities of enjoying themselves just because I am not married. It would not be fair to them."

"The only time that a young lady should be restricted from certain pleasures is if she has shown herself not to be responsible and or of not having good judgment," I furthered. "But if she is of sound mind, follows a sure morality, and can rely on her own independent judgment, then all is well."

"Also, for a young lady to be kept from the world just because her older sisters do not have husbands can lead to a half-life," Kitty compiled, "of her character not fully developing because she is kept too much away from the world for too long."

"I agree," Elena supported. "We humans develop from the experiences that we all have. If we are given no time to have experiences, then we can never learn from our mistakes. And as such, we come to men as half-women. We would not be good companions to them, because we are not even sure what our own characters are."

"Upon my word," Lady Catherine said, flabbergasted, "all of you do indeed give your opinions very decidedly, despite being such young people."

"We've had experiences," Elena stated. "And since we have, I'm afraid that there is no going back."

"No going back," Lady Catherine repeated, looking at Anne. "Yes, I do know a little bit about that."

We all continued to eat, waiting for Lady Catherine to find another topic that would suit her, and we didn't have long to wait.

"Well," Lady Catherine continued, "if I had been your mother, you Bennet girls would have been brought up very differently. You *all* would have learned to sing and play, as well as had been very accomplished artists. I still believe that your mother has much to answer for, and I will speak with her about it one day, for I do believe that she and I will meet. It will be inevitable."

We Bennet sisters looked at each other, each clearly getting an image of what it would be like for Mama and Lady Catherine to meet. It was not a pretty sight.

"But all that is over and done with now," Lady Catherine continued, "but if you ladies are going to be going to bathing-places, then I can do my duty and tell you how to prepare yourselves for sea-bathing, to keep from getting too brown, and making sure to maintain your health."

"Oh, that is very kind," Jane said, and this was encouragement enough. Lady Catherine began to give advice on everything about how a lady should properly sea-bathe. It took up all of dinner.

Afterwards, Lady Catherine ordered music to be performed. She arranged for Georgiana to play first, then I was second. This did not suit me at all, because Georgiana was clearly the better player by far. And then Lady Catherine had discovered that I could sing.

I begged her not to ask me to do so, due to being so inferior to Georgiana, but she was adamant. Mr. Darcy offered to join me, I let my courage grow, and I began to sing.

The surprise came when Mr. Darcy sang the male part of it. I looked up in shock as his beautiful baritone voice filled the air, and I was humbled. The man that I loved…could sing! Very beautifully as well.

With his voice added to mine and my playing, it turned a mediocre performance to a grand one. At the end of it all, Lady Catherine ordered Colonel Fitzwilliam and Darcy to play together, for it had been too long since she heard him play.

"You sing?" Kitty asked the Colonel.

"Yes," he responded, "but whether my sound is pleasant or not shall always be up for debate."

Colonel Fitzwilliam sat down to the pianoforte and began to play as both gentlemen began to sing. Dear god, they were beautiful!

Until that time, I never comprehended why watching us women play at instruments appealed to men, or why it charmed them. After all, we were merely playing music, and that was it. Now I stood corrected. There was something elegant and—sensuous—about watching the opposite sex perform so well at being accomplished. Both men appeared to be like a comet and be wondered at.

Instinctively, I turned to Jane, who could not remove her gaze from Colonel Fitzwilliam. I also noted Mr. Bingley looking a little apprehensive, and secretly, he must have been jealous. I recalled him marveling at how accomplished women were, indicating that he never learned to be musical himself. Now, he must have felt inadequate.

Eventually the gentlemen finished, and we all clapped so enthusiastically for them, having risen out of the spell that they cast on us.

"Most prodigious!" Jane exclaimed. "We are all so very amazed, for we never knew that you were such."

"Now I feel so very less in the eyes of the world," Kitty confessed, "for I had never had the ability to become accomplished when it comes to music. I am trying to learn now, but I fear that it is too late."

"I feel the same," Jane echoed. "There just always seemed as if there was something else that got in the way of learning, but now I have to confess that I just did not have the self-discipline to apply myself."

"Same with me," Mr. Bingley agreed, happy that they were the same in that way. "At least we are not alone in our inferiority to others."

"Misery loves company," Mr. Orwell said, "for those of us who lacked the talent can all at least find comfort in being one among many."

"Very much so," Anne said. "Too often I used my illness as an excuse for why I couldn't exert myself. But now, upon reflection, I was hiding behind my poor health."

"You were not hiding at all, Anne," Lady Catherine countered. "Your health was always affecting you, and you had no choice." She turned to us all. "Anne would have been a great proficient if her health had not been indifferent. Yes, she would have been. But since you are a married woman now, perhaps you will take up learning, for the sake of having an activity."

I brightened at this remark. For indeed, this was the first time that I heard her acknowledge her daughter's marriage. This acknowledgement was simple, but it also meant so much. It signified that she was growing to accept her daughter's marriage. This was very good, because we had not gotten the chance to talk about it before at all. Until that point, we had been quite left in the dark about it all. Sadly, due to the way the evening was structured, I did not get the chance to talk to Mr. Darcy about what had been discussed. Therefore, we parted that evening with just knowing that there was peace in the house.

CHAPTER 10

SOMETIMES THE RIGHT THING TO DO IS TO GIVE IN

The next day, I was composing a letter to send to Mama and Mary, when Mr. Darcy came upon me in the sitting room. The others were sitting on the other side of the room, listening to Lady Catherine.

"Elizabeth," he asked me, conspiratorially, "I was wondering if you would take a turn with me about the gardens."

"You know that I would love to," I responded eagerly.

"I was of the suspicion." He turned to Lady Catherine and announced that we were going for a walk along her shrubbery and gardens.

"What a splendid idea," Lady Catherine stated, "we should all go. Everyone, let us assemble in the vestibule once we are prepared. Step lightly!"

We obeyed and set out together. Lady Catherine headed up the excursion, and she lectured us all about the improvements in the garden and shrubbery of the ideas she had proposed to the gardener.

As she did so, Mr. Darcy and I lagged behind.

"I cannot go a moment further without knowing what happened," I augmented. "I must know."

"I know. And I myself am amazed at how things can work out so very well. At first, Lady Catherine was enraged, and she scolded them both with a fury. And you have seen my aunt when she is furious."

I chuckled. "Yes, I have. I would not wish her anger on my worst enemy. Actually, never mind, there is a wickedness about me, and I just might wish it on my worst enemy."

"After she had finished her lecture," Darcy continued, "Colonel Fitzwilliam and I managed to finally tell her that Mr. Orwell had married Anne without any consideration for her dowry or for Rosings Park. Eventually, she was given proof of this, especially since Mr. Orwell asked if he could maintain his post as the reverend at Hunsford, where he and Anne could live."

"He did?"

"Yes. He preferred to be a man of profession because that was what he was accustomed to. He was not a man of complete leisure. Of course, Lady Catherine refused to have Anne married to a man in trade. Mr. Orwell asked her to reconsider, but I do not believe that she will relent. I suppose, due to the inability to change the way events have unfolded, she had no choice but to accept."

"I never would have thought that I have seen the day where Lady Catherine accepted defeat."

"Well, she hasn't fully given up. She only accepted by allowing them to use 3,000 pounds a year after her death, so that they do not live to excess and learn to economize. Also, Colonel Fitzwilliam and I were made into Anne's financial advisors. If Anne informs us that Mr. Orwell is abusing her inheritance, or is mistreating her, we are allowed to interfere."

"You may not be her husband, but you will still be her protector," I said. "That is a perfectly suitable arrangement."

"I do owe them both that much."

"They are your family. I cannot help but enjoy how well all the matters have been resolved. Lady Catherine came to Brighton, all in a rage over our engagement. Only for her intended choice for you to elope, making it impossible for you to marry her, anyway. That gave Lady Catherine no choice but to accept me."

"So, this all could be construed as a happy accident."

"It could have all ended differently, I suppose. I am happy that it didn't." I looked up at him, with a smile in my eyes. "And I want to thank you, Mr. Darcy."

"Why so, I wonder?"

"Because we were unified. What I mean is that—well, you know how my parents were. When they married, they perhaps were in love. But quickly, that came undone, due to my mother being of a liberal mind that was very mean in understanding and wanted proper sense, and my father's attitude toward her changed over the years. Rather than trying to encourage her to improve her mind, he grew to be indifferent to her, and exposed her to the ridicule of her children. They were not happy, or unified. It is all well to disagree with one's spouse every now and again. Sometimes arguments can be a healthy thing. However, you can be of two minds, but one pairing, if both feel deeply for each other. And the way that you have been, you have included me in your decisions and made me feel as if I have a voice that means something to you. I will not take it lightly, you see. I admire that you make certain to make it feel as if we are a team. If that makes any sense."

"It makes a great deal of sense," he said, "and I appreciate that you notice my efforts. I want to be good for you."

"You are, as I want to be good for you. I just want you to know that I will never take you for granted."

"Do you swear to that, Lizzy? Do you promise?"

"Very much so."

We walked on with the group.

One day, as I was walking through the halls, Kitty and Elena were handing something to Dalton. It was a box that Kitty was asking to be sent.

"Can you make sure that it is treated with extra care?" Kitty asked. "If I need to pay for extra postage, then I will do so. I just need to make sure that it directly reaches that publisher. If it doesn't, then my whole life will feel like it is lost."

"I assure you that we shall arrange for it to be given special handling," Dalton said and then he left.

"Is that your novel?" I asked, walking up to them.

"Yes," Kitty answered. "Elizabeth, I am so scared. What if it gets lost in the mail or damaged? I have no choice but to send it, because it is the only way that it can be read. After all, seeing that it was from Rosings Park will increase the chances of publishers being impressed." Kitty took Elena's arm to steady herself. "But now I am so frightened. So terribly frightened."

"Kitty, if this publisher is foolish enough to not accept it, that is his shortcomings," I pointed out. "He has been given the proper postage in the parcel to send it back, correct?"

"Yes, I included the proper postage inside of the parcel."

"Well," Elena said, "Dalton seems to be a very reliable butler."

"I believe so," I agreed. "He will make sure that the package is treated with care. And since it comes from Rosings, the post will make certain that it does not get lost or damaged at all. I am also a little apprehensive, I will not deny. I worry about your book being so far away from you. And I am sorry that you never had the ability to have a copy of it with you."

"Writing a book is a strange sensation," Kitty added. "It is such a strange experience. Strange and indelicate as it is to say, but you begin to find your writing as like a child. My book is like a child that I have given birth to and now I am sending it away. I find it very hard. There is nothing so easy about parting with one's children. One feels very forlorn without them."

We walked to the drawing room to join the others. When we did so, I looked out the window and saw Jane walking with the Colonel. I couldn't help but watch them and see if there was any marked affection that was superior to Jane's feelings for Mr. Bingley, but there was no difference. Jane still felt everything deeply but kept it all within. Thus, it was still difficult to determine what she ever fully felt, and I was never going to ask her.

"I understand," Mr. Bingley asked us all, "that after this, you all mean to return to Longbourn."

"We do," Lydia answered for any of us first. The longer Lydia had remained in Rosings, the more Lydia realized that there was no place for her self-pity or hysterics. Lady Catherine naturally had such an imposing manner that Lydia lost her spiritedness around her, and it was nice to know that her intimidating demeanor was beneficial for something.

"Well," Mr. Bingley suggested, "I just wish to inform you all that I had written to the staff to be prepared for my coming, so Darcy and Miss Elena, Netherfield Park shall be ready for our coming there."

"Netherfield Park and Longbourn," Elena said. "I wonder what it is like. I cannot see that a place that you all grew up in can be anything else but pleasant," Elena said, looking around at us Bennets, "but it is so nice to be able to see new places. I am at the time of my life where novelty is always glamorous."

"I noticed that you do not write to your parents," Lady Catherine observed. "You have written no letters since coming here."

"Because my parents do not expect anything from me."

Lady Catherine squinted.

"Is that really so?" she asked. "Why not?"

"Well, your ladyship must understand that there are some things another lady would rather not share. We all have our terrifying secrets that haunt us. All that I can say is that I once fell in love with a man who proved to be unsuitable. He was not like you, Mr. Orwell, where he initially had good intentions. He did not. And suffice it to say that my parents cannot forgive me for how foolish I acted over my love for him."

"But you are not married now."

"Because my eyes were opened to the man he was. Eventually, he repented his villainy, but I was not like Mrs. Orwell. Things did not end so beautifully."

Lady Catherine raised an eyebrow and then she leaned back in her seat.

"And you all really must leave tomorrow?" she asked.

"It is best," Kitty replied. "Our mother must miss us terribly."

"Well, your mother surely can spare you, for she still has one of her daughters at home."

"With our father gone," I finalized, "it is best that we return, madam. She will want us home."

"I cannot deny that I would prefer it if you stayed. You all make such an interesting set of people. Rosings Park will be emptier without you."

"There is a simple remedy for that," Lydia inferred, "you really ought to invite us again."

"Lydia," I chided.

"Such impertinence," Lady Catherine snapped at her. "But I understand your eagerness to return, Miss Lydia, and you must be sad yourself for going away. It is natural that your attachment to Rosings has increased. It is only logical. And yes, it would be better if you come. You must all come a few times a year. I shall send invitations for you to return in three months' time. Yes, you all will come. Yes."

We did not argue, but steadily agreed.

The next day, it was time to leave for Longbourn. Our departure from Rosings Park was much more agreeable than how we entered it.

"She is keeping me at Rosings," Charlotte said, "which I am happy for. I did not want to return home and be a burden again. If I did, I would feel like all my chances would end. And that would be the last thing that I wished."

"Charlotte, when will you see that you are not a burden?" I questioned.

"When it stops being true. But I am happy that I am of some use here. Even if I am here because Lady Catherine needs someone to lecture and rule over, I can bear it all so very well. I find that I can bear such temper very easily."

"You were able to bear Mr. Collins, god rest his soul, so I am of the mind that you can not only survive Rosings Park, but you can thrive here."

"Give my love to my parents and family," she said. "And tell Maria that Lady Catherine is amenable to her coming to visit."

"I shall."

"I write it in my letters to them, but I am not certain that Maria has recovered from the last time she came here."

"She enjoyed it," I assured her. "Believe me, she found it to be the most wonderful thing she had undergone. And I do believe that all shall be well. After all, there are no more people here to elope and make things interesting for you."

"I retire to monotony," Charlotte said, "and I am so happy for it."

She, Mrs. Jenkinson, Mr. and Mrs. Orwell waved their farewells with Lady Catherine as our carriages departed.

"Oh, home," Lydia sighed. "I cannot wish for us to return there!"

"Do you want us to tell Mama what occurred in Brighton?" I asked.

Lydia's face distorted, terrified.

"Elizabeth, you wouldn't dare."

"I would not," I said, "because I want to believe that you will tell her, in your own time. But one thing that I do ask in return."

"What?"

"Behave."

Lydia rolled her eyes and looked out the window.

"Why is it so wrong to have fun?"

"There is nothing wrong with having fun," Jane countered. "What is wrong is when others get hurt so that you can obtain it."

We journeyed on.

CHAPTER 11

LONGBOURN LOST

*H*ertfordshire appeared on the horizon, and we first travelled to Longbourn.

"Our house will not be grand or impressive when you first see it," Kitty said to Elena, "but it is very comfortable and suited our needs."

"Never fear," Elena said, "I've had enough of large homes and the scandals that occur within them to satisfy my curiosity for quite some time."

"Large homes and scandals that occur in them?" Kitty repeated. "I like that."

"You may use it."

"Thank you."

We rolled down the lane where our home rested at the end of it, and there it was.

"Home," I voiced. "I knew that I would miss it, but I did not think of how much until now."

"There are few things that luxury cannot erase or defeat," Jane said. "This moment is one of them."

Suddenly, the door burst open, and Mama emerged out of it, with Mary behind her.

"And the image is completed," Kitty stated.

"How long it's been!" Mama cried. "How long it has been!"

106

"And that is our mother and sister," Kitty told Elena. "Mrs. Bennet and Mary."

We all disembarked from the carriages, and Mama was beside herself.

"All my daughters returned to me at last," she cried, embracing us all. "How I missed you. It was cruel of you to be gone from me for so long, so very cruel. You must not do such again, except for Lizzy of course, because she is married to the greatest man in England." Here Mama turned to Mr. Darcy.

"Mrs. Bennet," Mr. Darcy stated, "it is a pleasure to see you once more."

"I..." Mama broke off, awed by him. "Mr. Darcy, you could knock me down with a feather. Never would I have expected my daughter to meet with such good fortune in making the greatest match in all the land. I am happy to call you my son. And it is so nice to have a son. Oh dear, I am saying all the wrong things." She turned to Mr. Bingley. "Mr. Bingley!"

"I can see the surprise in your eyes," Mr. Bingley noted. "I hope that you can bear the sight of me."

"I can indeed, most ardently," she cried. "It is good to see you again. I was worried that you would quit Netherfield Park entirely, so this is good news indeed." She gave Jane a knowing look, Jane blushed and looked down at the floor. Colonel Fitzwilliam saw the hope in Mama's eyes, and it humbled him.

"And allow me to introduce my sister and my cousins," Mr. Darcy continued. "This is my sister, Miss Georgiana Darcy. And these are my cousins, Colonel Fitzwilliam, second son to my uncle, the Earl of Matlock, and Miss Elena Darcy, daughter to my other uncle on my father's side."

"You all are very welcome to Longbourn, I am sure. Now do come inside. I have prepared refreshments and I should also inform you all that I have arranged for a dinner party here tomorrow evening, to celebrate my dear Lizzy's engagement. I trust you all can come, seeing as you have no previous engagements."

"We shall look forward to it, very much so," Mr. Bingley affirmed. "And I suppose that it would be proper for me to have a dinner party as well, at Netherfield. And since I have the lovely Miss Georgiana and Miss Elena here to serve as hostesses, I hope that the people of Hertfordshire will forgive me for being such a prodigal child."

"I am certain that they will all be happy to see you," Mama said as we entered the vestibule and removed our pelisses, gloves, and bonnets. "When word was sent around that you and Mr. Darcy were returning, the whole town became more alive with excitement. And that you have brought more family with you! Now they all will love you forever."

We entered the sitting room and Hill and the other servants brought in tea.

"You all cannot imagine how happy I am that you all are home," Mama repeated. "Mr. Darcy, Mr. Bingley, Colonel, Miss Darcy, and Miss Elena, ever since their father has passed away, you cannot imagine how hard it is to part with one's children. It is not easy at all."

"We did not mean to stay away so long," Jane assured her. "And we were happy to be home."

"Very happy," Lydia cried, taking Mama's hand. "But I must tell you that I have had such a mighty adventure! I have seen so much, Mama."

"We all have," Kitty added, "but before we do, how have you all been?"

"We have been experiencing good weather and good company," Mary replied, "and people have asked us every week about your adventures and traveling all over England."

"The best thing of traveling is returning home," I added.

"But that cannot be the end of your stories," Mama urged. "We must hear everything! For it will give us such a comfort to hear happy things, especially after knowing that Longbourn is lost to us."

We all froze in our seats, shocked.

"Mama," Mary corrected, "that is our own woes and ought not to be discussed with strangers."

"Oh, hush dear! After all, they are not mere strangers, but are family now. There is no need to conceal anything from them, especially since all of Hertfordshire knows our situation."

"Please clarify," I pressed, impatient. "Did you just say that Longbourn was lost?"

"Yes," Mama said heavily. "It is better that you all know now."

"Uncle Philips discovered another heir to inherit Longbourn," Mary narrated. "Since Longbourn is entailed to the next male relation to father, he was obligated to search our family records. The legality of the documents expressly ordered this, therefore, he was bound. He did stumble on the next to inherit. Our father's half-sister married and had a son."

"Half-sister?" I asked.

"Our grandfather's daughter under his first marriage."

"Your father's father had been married twice," Mama informed us. "Your grandfather had a daughter before he ever had your father, which was under a second marriage."

"We were never told of this," I uttered.

"Because your father never even knew his older sister!" she spat, getting more enraged with each moment that she spoke. "You see, your grandfather's first wife died in childbirth. Being a widower who was constantly working to maintain his estate, and not having a mother to tend to the child, his first wife's family offered to take the child and raise her themselves. Understanding that this was the best course of action for the child, since there were many women in his late wife's family who were experienced at raising children, he agreed. Another detail to this arrangement was that the daughter would be given her mother's last name, rather than Bennet. Your grandfather was eager to accept, and the young infant was given the name of Jenna MacMillan, which was her mother's family. She was raised by them and has never been to England a day in her life. A few years later, your grandfather married again, and had a son who inherited Longbourn. Oh, if we had a son, then all would have been well. Why could we not have had a son?"

"Mama, do not distress yourself," Jane coaxed her. "Please. It cannot be changed, so we must accept."

"But if I had done my duty, and gave your father a son, then we would not be in this complication."

"Madam," Elena interrupted, "I do not mean to speak on family matters that are not my business, but since you have asked the question, I feel at liberty to do so. No woman or man can control what their child is born as. It is out of anyone's hands."

"Very true," Lydia said. "We cannot change this. And we like who we are! And does it occur to you that it hurts us to hear you talk about it so much?"

"Quiet, you silly girl."

"They are correct," I pressed. "Mama, you forget yourself. Besides, you mentioned something. You have told us that we had a great aunt this entire time, but that she has never stepped foot in England before."

"Yes," Kitty said, "that part was what puzzled me. If she has never been to England, then that means that she and Father could have spent their entire lives and never met once. Our grandfather perhaps never even told his son that he had a sister before."

"It would make sense that he didn't, since there was a strong possibility that he would never see his wife's family again," Mary inferred.

"Why?" I asked. "How far are they? Do they reside in Scotland or Ireland?"

"Further. The MacMillans live in America."

"America?" Mr. Bingley repeated, shocked. "Really?"

"Yes," Mary continued. "It seems that our grandfather had travelled to America, on holiday, met his first wife, married her, brought her here to Longbourn, and she passed away so soon in their marriage, due to the pains of childbirth."

"The shortage of their marriage could explain why no one remembers this first marriage here," I deduced. "No one got the chance to know this woman, and that must have broken our grandfather's heart."

"As indelicate as this is to say," Mr. Darcy admitted, "it is perhaps best that the wife's family took the child in."

"Why?" I asked, hurt.

"Because a man who has just lost his wife is not always in the best mental state to raise a child. Not all men have the strength to recover so quickly from a devastation. Your grandfather perhaps saw himself as giving his daughter her best chance at a family."

"And what became of our great Aunt, Jenna?" Jane asked.

"She grew up to get married and have a large family. Three sons and two daughters. They all reached adulthood before she fell ill and passed away herself. Her eldest son, Mr. Wyatt Nelson, is thirty-two years old, and is now the sole inheritor of Longbourn."

"Our Uncle Philips discovered all this?" Kitty asked. "How could he find records that were that extensive?"

"He didn't," Mary said, going over to the desk and pulled out a letter.

"He discovered our grandfather's first child but wrote to the family on our behalf to explain the situation. They wrote back to us to explain the history of Jenna Macmillan's lineage, and we discovered that she married a Mr. Claude Nelson, and they had five children, who survive them both."

"Thus making this Mr. Wyatt Nelson a complete stranger to us who will now be the proud owner of Longbourn and drive us out of our deserved home." Mama pressed her lips together, but her eyes were teary. "It breaks my heart. It breaks my heart indeed."

"What does the letter say?" Mr. Bingley asked. "Surely, this Mr. Nelson will be sensitive about inheriting an estate from ladies who have grown up there. There are certain people who are sensitive to such delicate situations. This Mr. Nelson might be one of those people."

"Mr. Bingley, not everyone is as kindhearted as you!" Mama cried. "He wrote back in the letter that he will come to Longbourn in two months' time to see the estate that was his to inherit and meet us all."

"I am very sorry," Georgiana offered. "This is a very tragic thing indeed."

"And do not advise me to hold my tongue at all," Mama said to

Jane and me. "Hertfordshire is aware of our situation and has been aware of Longbourn being lost to us for some time. I am not being uncouth for mentioning it, but rather I wanted to be the first one to tell you this news myself."

She covered her mouth and looked away from us, while Jane rushed to her and held her shoulders, trying to calm her down.

"Mary," I asked, "can I read the letter?"

Mary handed it to me, and I quickly read over it.

"Yes," I concluded. "Indeed, he is coming in two months. But his manner of writing appears to be kindhearted. He is aware of the indelicacy of the business, and desires to meet us, for the sake of connecting with relatives of his that he was not aware that he had. He also is viewing this as a holiday since he has never been to Britain. Perhaps he is not vicious, we must hope."

"But we do not know that," Mama whined. "What ever brings an American here? He has no reason to come, since he will not ever be well-regarded. They are as strange to our customs as we are to theirs and cannot begin to understand the refinements of our society. They would appear as vulgar and crass."

I bit my lip—Mama had no notion that she was describing herself. Or how offensive she sounded.

"We visit America," I said, "so why can they not come here?"

"There will be no one like him here," she continued, "and so it is best that he remains where he is and never come. What a vicious and mercenary man! Odious monster. If he had any goodness in him, then he would not wish to quit the society that tolerates him and had just sent a letter leaving Longbourn to us, though it is in his name."

"Mama," I furthered, finishing the letter, "we cannot judge him now because the letter is sanguine. What I mean is that he does not write with any overt intentions to take Longbourn once he gets here and forsake us. There is the chance that he will be lenient. Let us not judge him until he comes. If he does prove to be the worst of men, then you are at liberty to disparage him."

"Precisely," Mary confirmed. "Mama, I have often told you that it is best not to judge anyone before meeting them."

"It would do better to be kind to him when he comes," Jane offered, "because if he likes us, he might feel a tenderness to us."

"And it is not like we are without friends, of course," Kitty pointed out, "our aunt and uncle would not leave us on the street to starve."

"And too many people love us!" Lydia boasted. "We will always have friends. Well, I know that *I* will."

"You are the worst," Mary whispered to Lydia.

"Very true. We are not alone," Mama said, taking my hand. "Dearest Lizzy, I never thought you would be the one to save us all, but it is the best sort of surprise." She looked at Mr. Darcy. "Mr. Darcy, Elizabeth shall make you a fine wife, and I do not believe that you could have made a better choice. And having friends is very good at a time like this. For without them, we are quite forlorn."

I blushed, so very ashamed at our mother's behavior, and Mr. Darcy nodded, not knowing what to do. Also, Lydia was still being Lydia, not fully enhancing her character, and she and Mary bickered. It was all so very painful to show that our family was like this.

"Well," Colonel Fitzwilliam furthered, not pained by what he saw, "you have two months before this man comes, and when he does, your daughters are all very correct. He might very well be congenial and is merely curious about his newfound family. It is always best to respect someone until they prove to be unworthy of that respect. You clearly are not without friends, and there always seems to be hope on the horizon."

"Oh, you are all so very kind!" Mama declared. "I do not know when I have ever encountered a group of new acquaintances who have been so understanding and engaging. It takes my breath away. And I am honored that you all come to visit my home. Yes, I am truly honored! Indeed, I feel better already."

Soon, Mr. Darcy, Mr. Bingley, Colonel Fitzwilliam, Georgiana, and Elena had to leave to go to Netherfield, but Mama pressed them to promise to come tomorrow evening—something they already agreed to.

I felt my cheeks burn with embarrassment. Indeed, I worried that Mr. Darcy would break off our engagement in the dead of night. Before he left with the group, I gave him one last look of shame, but he returned it with a look of reassurance and gentleness, putting my heart at rest. He still loved me, and there was nothing to worry over.

At last, they left, and I could breathe a sigh of relief.

"What were you all trying to do?" I asked Mama, Mary, and Lydia. "Scare them away with your overbearing manners and offensiveness? They perhaps now find us to be the most vulgar people in the world."

"They do not," Lydia retorted.

"Lizzy, you cannot speak to me in such a way, and you know that," Mama said. "Besides, it all came about in such a natural way, that I daresay they were happy that we were so honest. I am always right about these sorts of things."

Jane gave me a sympathetic look and we all unpacked our things, then went down to supper.

CHAPTER 12

THE JOYS & PAINS OF HAVING A MOTHER
LIKE OURS

The next day, we received a letter, hand-delivered by Mr. Darcy. It was an invitation from Mr. Bingley, inviting us all to a dinner at Netherfield Park on next Thursday. Ten major families had been invited and we were among them. When Mr. Darcy arrived, he handed Mama the invitation and she professed her joy for twenty minutes, often repeating how this invitation gave us something to look forward to. When she finished, she turned her attention to the wedding.

"Now for the wedding," Mama began, "oh, this is so very exciting. I have many ideas for the best gowns and flowers to have for the arrangement. And you will be married at Longbourn church, of course."

"Madam," Mr. Darcy stated simply. "I do not mean to contradict you, for I can very well understand your desire for your daughter to be married here, where all your family's friends can witness our desirable event. Yet, being the Master of Pemberley makes me obligated to marry in Derbyshire, at the parsonage on my estate. Please, I do hope that you understand that this is something I owe to the county."

Mama brought her hand to her chest. "Oh, I do understand that. Of course, every mother wants to see their child married in the village they were raised in, but Mr. Darcy, I would never deny you this right. Such a great man as yourself! Some customs must be adhered to. And this will give me the chance to see Pemberley. Oh, now I am all aglow at the prospect of seeing so great a home. I shall grow quite distracted."

"Shall I play some music?" Mary asked.

"Not at the moment, dear," Mama said, "but perhaps later, Mr. Darcy would enjoy the pleasure of hearing you. My daughters are my pride and joy, Mr. Darcy, and they are so accomplished. But you have known that already and were very clever to spot it. My dear Elizabeth is witty and clever herself. Her father always boasted of her quickness of mind. I didn't notice what her father meant..." She pressed her handkerchief over her mouth. "Oh, my dear late Mr. Bennet...but you did notice it as well. I am happy that you were more keen-sighted than I."

"Intelligence in a woman is a wonderful thing," Mr. Darcy stated, "but it often is not treasured too highly by some. I have often noticed that people do not encourage women to exercise their own style of wit, so it is not your fault. I am only happy that I had the good fortune to be taught the reverse of what others preach."

"Yes. Yes, yes, yes. Now, let us talk of plans for the wedding."

"Mama," Jane requested, "the grounds of Longbourn look so well at this time of year. Elizabeth wants to show it to Mr. Darcy, and I would love to talk of the wedding plans with you."

"Yes," I pressed, "Jane knows my taste very well."

Mama agreed to this readily and Mr. Darcy and I found the joys of a quick retreat.

"So," I said as we walked in the gardens, our arms linked, "seeing you arrive here gave me all the hope and joy that it could, rather than a letter sent breaking off our engagement."

"You thought that I would reject you on the grounds of having a mother such as yours?" he asked, smiling.

"Yes, I did worry," I said, laughing, "a part of me shall always worry about losing you."

"Then that part of you need never do so," he assured me. "You and I have been to the edge of every experience together. What crisis can we not face?"

"I think the easier question that would present the shorter list is what crisis have we not faced already?"

"Precisely. Your father passed away, Wickham proposed to you, I had to win your heart, we have my sister who will always be recovering from Wickham's desertion, I helped create a tangled triangle of love between Mr. Bingley, Colonel Fitzwilliam and Jane, Miss Bingley fell into an hysteria over us, my cousin appeared out of nowhere and needed my protection, my aunt tried to dissolve our engagement, my cousin eloped with her clergyman, and now we are here. After all the abysses that we have endured, why would I leave you now?"

"We are very much together on facing the future, come what may."

"Yes, come what may."

"But please tell Mr. Bingley, Elena, Georgiana, and the colonel that we apologize for our mother's behavior. And Lydia and Mary's bickering. I know how it must make us look."

"After all that we have undergone, it makes you all appear as a family that is no different than ours. Your mother, ironically, displayed no less crassness than my aunt. There is no shame that she could cast on you that we have endured ourselves. Richard, Bingley, Georgiana, Elena, and I have all now experienced the vulgarity of our family members. Also, your mother was correct. When we settled into Netherfield, I overheard many of the servants talking. They all know about Longbourn being lost to a distant American relation, and often we are given the principle of religion but are left to practice its principles in a way where we are afraid of foreigners. And your mother's hysterics were also a natural reaction to seeing her family again and feeling at liberty to share her misery of losing her home."

"Am I going mad, or are you judging my mother in a kinder light?"

"You are going mad."

I pinched him.

"Oh, very well," he elaborated, "despite that I do not know if I could bear your mother's company for too long, I am now putting her behavior into perspective… and I liked that she fell into that topic of discussion so easily. It gave me an excuse to not talk very much. She and I have little in common, but when it comes to estates, we all share the same anxieties. Also, I have another set of news."

"News, oh! That thing that makes all eyebrows raise."

"And this one will raise both eyebrows. Mr. Bingley and my valets have arranged for all invitations to be re-directed to Netherfield Park, while we were at Rosings. We knew, no matter the outcome of those events, that we would return here soon. Well, there is always a little bit of eagerness when lovers are involved. When we arrived, there were already letters waiting for us."

"You mentioned lovers. Am I to presume that you are referring to Sir Aleck Granger?"

"Yes, my shrewd love. The one and the same. He asked us if he could break his journey with us, while also not being ashamed to desire this visit only if Elena was still in our company."

"Yes, true lovers do move quickly. How do you wish to reply?" I asked.

"I am not against it. Sir Aleck is a great man, and it appears as if Elena enjoys his company. But I was not certain of to what extent is her feelings for him."

"Would you prefer if I were to ask her how deep are her preferences for his company? And once I find out her feelings toward him, then you can decide how to reply."

"Yes, that was precisely what I wished. That would help me a great deal."

"It would be my pleasure," I assured him. "Also, how is Elena regarding her family? Have they written to her at all?"

"Not that I am aware of. I know they received my letters to them about my taking charge of her, and they wrote back, accepting this, but that is the last that I heard of them. Elena does not seem to care."

"Perhaps she does and has not wished to trouble us over it."

As we walked around the house, we saw Kitty sitting alone in the drawing room, writing her novel.

"I marvel at Miss Kitty," he said, "for I do not understand how she can tolerate Miss Elena's company with such equanimity, knowing that Sir Aleck prefers Elena than to herself."

"I can only assume that Kitty felt deeply for Sir Aleck but was not in love with him. Therefore, she was not so far into the middle of her affections, that she could not extradite herself from them. Also, I have the suspicion that she fell in love with her writing first, and it may very well always be her first love. So, she had something else to rely upon to establish her own self-importance, rather than relying upon a man's affections, who had placed his affections elsewhere. Either way, she is very heroic in her own fashion. I marvel at her ability to be friends with Elena as well."

We spent a great deal of time in the shrubbery, then at last we retreated to the woods that abutted Longbourn. Eventually, we were far removed from the eyes of any looker-on and gave into our passions. Closing the space between us, we exchanged another long and deep kiss.

Mr. Darcy remained with us the entire day, even throughout Mama's preparations for the dinner party and our having to retire to our rooms to change for dinner. Eager to be the first to finish getting dressed so that I could join him again, I let my hair remain the same, then I raced back downstairs, to be met by Hill, who was rushing about, meeting Mama's demands.

"Hill, have you seen Mr. Darcy?" I asked.

"He is in the library," she responded. "Mrs. Bennet advised that he would be happiest in there while everyone got ready for the evening."

"He is in Father's library?" I asked, startled by the coincidence of it.

"Yes, Miss Elizabeth."

"Thank you."

Walking to Papa's library, I turned the knob gently and silently entered. Mr. Darcy's back was to me as he sat in father's chair, reading one of Father's books.

In that instant, an image of father reading flashed before my eyes, and I saw a split infinity before me. On the one hand, I saw father, reading away as he always had. On the other hand of that infinity, I saw Mr. Darcy there, sitting in the same fashion, enjoying a book in his hand.

Sensing my presence, he turned around and lowered the book.

"Elizabeth, you look beautiful."

"Thank you," I replied, serene. "You remind me of him now. Of Father. For a moment, I thought that I saw him still here, alive and well."

"I get the sense that he would not fancy the idea of me reading his books."

"He would have wanted someone to appreciate them." Walking up to him, I reached out my hand and he took it, kissing my fingers.

"Elizabeth!" Mama cried. "Where are you?"

"Coming, Mama," I replied. "I wonder what she could need me for. Stay in here and you will be safe from the pains of having to confront party arrangements."

I left him alone, where he returned to his book.

Soon guests arrived and Darcy lined up with us to meet them all. To see him there, among us, was such a shocking turn of events. Once we all thought him to despise our lowly sphere in society, and now here we were, joined by family struggles.

The Netherfield party were the first to arrive, then the Philips came, the Lucases, the Longs and the Hales.

"Sir William and Lady Lucas," Jane said, "we are happy to inform you all that Charlotte sends her love, and she is still very happy at Rosings Park."

"Oh, of course she is," Sir William responded, "I knew that my daughter made such a fortunate alliance when she married Mr. Collins, for he came with such incredible connections."

Mama gave him a look.

"Of course, I only enjoyed the alliance because Mr. Collins was the reverend of Lady Catherine de Bourgh and no more than that. I knew that my daughter would be exposed to the best in life."

"But as for any other advantages that the match had to bestow other than Charlotte's happiness," Lady Lucas smoothed over, "those were never really desired."

"Indeed so, indeed so."

"But I wish to know more about Brighton!" Mrs. Long said. "I know that it was too cold to go sea-bathing, but is there anything else about it that is worth seeing besides that?"

"You have never been to Brighton, Mrs. Long?" I asked. "I never knew."

"Yes, sadly, I am not as worldly as I wished that I could be. I never got the chance to see the world. And when you get married there never seems to be enough time in the day."

"Precisely," Aunt Philips added, "when you marry, you think that your life opens up to more adventures, but then the weight of responsibility comes pouring in."

"Oh, I know that look," Uncle Philips responded, "and that tone of voice."

"And what does that mean, Mr. Philips?"

"It means that you secretly want me to take you on a holiday somewhere, and you wish for me to stumble on the idea one day, despite that it was really your idea the entire time."

Everyone laughed.

"That is the trick of marriage," Aunt Philips advised to Elena, who sat beside her. "Always having good ideas and making the other spouse believe that they were the ones who had it all along."

"A paltry trick!" Uncle Philips countered.

"A generous one though," Elena responded, "it offers genius sometimes, when genius was not present before."

"Oh dear, our women are becoming wise and intelligent," Mr. Long commented. "We cannot have that, or we men will never be able to take control again."

"Do you really want control when it comes to house management?" Aunt Philips responded. "As long as economy is being practiced, I always found it wiser and safer to do what we women tell you to do."

"For that is the sure way of being a man who makes it to an old age and is still healthy," Sir William observed. "Remember, young men: happy wife, happy life."

"Since I am on my way to becoming a married man," Mr. Darcy considered, "I suppose that I am the only young man here who can apply your maxim to my habit."

"Mr. Darcy, you were already practicing that maxim," I pointed out.

"Good," he responded. "I was hoping you would tell them such, because I do not think they would have believed me if I had told them so."

The dinner passed in such the amusing way where all casually enjoyed themselves. After dinner, the men separated to the other room, while we women conversed with each other.

"Well," Mrs. Long said, "now that the men are gone, we can talk freely."

"I can assure you," Kitty responded to her, "that I was doing that already."

"When they return, the men shall not part us, I am determined. We want none of them, do we?"

"Why do you say that?"

"Because they are such an entirely different species to us. They rarely offer conversation that is appealing to hear."

"You speak so bitterly, Mrs. Long," Kitty realized. "What is the reason for this?"

"Nothing more than general observations."

"You would not want me to give into general observations, would you? That just seems like a recipe for my own undoing."

Soon, the men returned, and Mama arranged for cards to be played. At my table was Mr. Darcy, Jane, Mr. Bingley, the Lucases, and Elena. I noticed, throughout the evening, that Mama had specifically arranged for Jane and Mr. Bingley to be always next to each other, and this was so evident.

I only wondered if Colonel Fitzwilliam would regard this as an accident, or if he was beginning to see that Mama was aglow with another scheme of hers.

Overall, the dinner party ended so very well, and Mama was so happy when everyone had departed.

"Oh, it feels just like it did when your poor father was alive," she cried. "I do not believe that the evening could have gone better. The food was perfect. Surely, it was superior to the Lucases. Elizabeth, I do believe that Mr. Darcy was happy. He appeared as such. Was he?"

"Yes, he was," I gathered, "he enjoyed himself very much."

"I even saw him smile a couple of times," Mary said. "That is not a common thing for him to do, is it?"

"No, it's not. Mama, he loved the evening, and you did it very well."

"And does he like me yet? I know that he must remember when I didn't like him. But I had no choice but to despise him, as you recall. He slighted you and I did not like that. But surely, he sees that I am trying to be better now. Do you think he is beginning to become more open to my company?"

"I do believe that he is. I enjoy that you wish for him to like you. As long as you maintain a strong sense of propriety, I do believe that my fiancé will one day be excited to see you."

Lydia snorted.

"What is it, dear?" Mama asked.

"Nothing."

"She is just jealous," Mary noted.

"Am not."

"Are too."

"Am not."

"Are too. And recall that envy is one of the most dangerous of sins."

"Quiet, the both of you," Mama ordered. "Sometimes I wonder if you both will be arguing forever."

"Well, they are very good at it," Kitty said, yawning. "I would be surprised if they turned it into a good sport."

"We are all tired," Mama said, "and we are speaking nonsense." She turned to Jane. "Jane, I do not understand your situation at all.

Mr. Bingley leaves, and no engagement forms between you both. Then you return home and Mr. Bingley is in the company. But you are not engaged? How can that be?"

"That is something that only Mr. Bingley knows," Jane said, "and it would be better not to inquire. Well, he is here now, and that is all that matters. Mark my words, by the end of the week, you shall see that Mr. Bingley and I will be common and friendly acquaintances."

"I do not understand," she said. "I do not understand anything." Mama touched my hand. "Thank God, you did everything you could to get Mr. Darcy. Now we are all saved."

Mama called for Hill as she went upstairs to get ready to retire.

I gave Jane a look and she breathed out.

"She does not understand that you are not the first one to get married," I explained. "Her mind is suffering from being overturned by the shock of not correctly foreseeing the future."

"I know," Jane said, "I just wish that she would not have placed that burden on me."

"I did not know that it affected you."

"I never showed it." She smiled, tapped my shoulder, bade us all goodnight, and went upstairs.

"I never thought that I would say this," Kitty put in, "but there is something comfortable about being born in the middle. It can be more likely that no one has any expectations of you."

"Or it can lead to being invisible sometimes," Mary said, "but I have learned to use that to advantage."

"There's a reason that you are invisible sometimes, Mary." Lydia laughed, tugging at Mary's sleeve before she went upstairs. "You choose to be."

"That's what I said," Mary replied, leaving the room as well.

"I am fine with being the youngest," Lydia cried.

"Yes, all of Hertfordshire knows that you are."

They kept bickering as they left, followed by Kitty, who stood up.

"I thought things would be different," I remarked, following her out of the room.

"What do you mean?"

"I thought after her heartache, that Lydia would have changed."

"There are some things that you cannot control. Lydia will be as Lydia will be. That is just the way of it. She might need to grow and develop on her own accord. That's what I did. Either way, do not distress yourself on matters that you cannot control. That's how you lead to making yourself ill."

CHAPTER 13

THE ULTIMATE DECISION

The next day, we all were excited for the party at Netherfield Hall.

"I do not believe that hope is lost," Mama said. "I feel that this party is still in compliment to you, Jane."

"It is in honor of Lizzy and Darcy's engagement," Jane said. "There is no way I can pretend that I am of special regard. But thank you for believing for me." She kissed Mama on the cheek and sipped only a little bit of tea.

"Remember to only sip as little tea as possible," Mama advised. "We don't want to have to leave early. For, with any hope, there might be a little bit of dancing after the dinner."

"Oh, I long to dance," Lydia wailed.

"As do I," Kitty echoed the sentiments.

"Jane and Elizabeth, can you persuade Mr. Bingley to allow us to dance?"

"Between Georgiana, Aunt Philips, and Mary, we have enough women to play for us."

"Oh, I shall be called on again," Mary remarked, acting set upon.

"You know that you enjoy it," Mama rebuked. "Mary, if you are going to be regarded as the most accomplished woman in the county, then you had better be willing to show it every now and again."

Mary couldn't help but smile to herself.

As the day continued, we all were aflutter, preparing for the dinner party, with an express desire to look our best. When we finished, it felt as if we were going to the Netherfield Ball again, despite that there was no ball—and father was not there with us.

At six o'clock, our carriage set out to Netherfield Park, and the Bingleys and Darcys were waiting for us, along with the Colonel. Since Netherfield was much larger than Longbourn, Bingley could invite a couple more families, so the Hanleys, Stills, Fairfaxes and Earnshaws were also present.

Mr. Bingley was very kind, arranging for me to sit next to Mr. Darcy. While he sat at the head, however, he could not help but have Jane seated next to him but was diplomatic enough to have the Colonel sit on her other side, followed by Kitty, who sat next to the Colonel. This gave Jane the right to speak with both men whenever she wished, and Kitty and the Colonel got along very well, so he would never feel rejected.

"How is Jane feeling about that?" Darcy asked me.

"I am certain that she is in inner turmoil, while also being happier than ever. She likes them both, so she is happy to be near them, but also she does not like that she causes them both pain. In moments like this, I am reminded of what my father would say."

"What?"

"Next to being married, being tossed in love is the next best thing. It gives a woman distinction amongst her companions."

"He really believed that?"

"He did. Or at least, he was very good at making it appear as if he did believe it, and we should believe it. Dear Father."

"You reminisce."

"Maybe he was correct. There is something to be said about having experiences regarding love, loss, and romance, before you do marry. You come to the last one with more experience, and more developed. If we had married soon after we had met, I believe that we would have driven each other mad."

He chuckled at this.

"Yes," he agreed, "we were not complete yet."

"And had not undergone enough trials and tribulations of the heart. But when we did finally agree on the happiest alliance ever, we had overcome all the silliness, and now can avoid it altogether. By the way, my mother wishes for you to like her."

He slanted me a glance. "Does she?"

"Yes. I just thought it best to tell you, so that I can warn you."

"Warn me?"

"She will try to make up for all the times that she was disagreeable to you. As a result, she will try too hard, and that will embarrass you. I am sorry."

"I understand."

The dinner past very well, and as we retired to the other room, Mr. Bingley addressed us all.

"Everyone," he announced, "I understand that it is necessary for men and women to retreat to two separate rooms at this time, but Miss Bennet and Miss Kitty were talking about the idea of dancing, and I quickly realized that I wished to dance as well. Would anyone be willing to be kind to their host and invite a dance?"

"I am of the mind to do so!" Lydia cried. "And I will make one of the Lucas boys stand up with me."

"They are all very willing to agree to that arrangement," Sir William Lucas encouraged.

Everyone agreed to the idea of it, chairs were pulled back and Georgiana offered to play—much to the furtive vexation of Mary, who had wanted to play first.

For the first time, all the families had young men in their party, and the males outnumbered the females. That was a rarity indeed.

As a result, there was always the women dancing, but there were always some men sitting down. Being the engaged set, Mr. Darcy and I led the dance, with Mr. Bingley choosing Jane, Colonel Fitzwilliam choosing Kitty as a second option, and the women feeling the joys of finally having a bountiful choice of partners.

We danced the first set, and it was marvelous.

"You are smiling as we dance," I professed.

"I smile because you smile."

"Finally, I do something that is properly infectious. Now the question is who will you dance with next?" I asked. "Before we leave Hertfordshire, I want everyone to love you here. What better way than for you to dance with another Hertfordshire lady?"

"You are assigning another partner for me?"

"Never! You can choose your next partner yourself, and it cannot be one of the Netherfield residents. Dance with someone who you are not familiar with. Be brave, Mr. Darcy. You are a hero so often, that surely you know how to rise to the occasion."

"Very well." He considered this for a time. "I shall ask Maria Lucas to stand up with me."

"I am sure that you will find her charming." As we danced, I sneakily stole a kiss on his cheek.

"You wicked creature," he commented.

"You cannot escape being married to me now."

The dance came to an end, and we applauded.

———

"Well," Mary said heavily, who had not been used to dancing so rigorously, "I daresay that I would not be proper if I continued to enjoy the dance while Miss Darcy is tied to the pianoforte. Miss Darcy, I would be perfectly willing to exchange places."

"Thank you," Georgiana said, "for I would like to dance."

"Then might I be too presumptuous for asking for your hand this time, Miss Darcy?" Mr. John Lucas asked, who was seventeen.

"I accept," Miss Darcy replied, taking his hand as Mary took her place at the instrument.

"And Miss Maria," Darcy appealed, "would you be willing to dance with me?"

Maria's mouth dropped open.

"Yes—yes—yes," Maria stuttered. "I would be delighted." Maria gave me a look.

"Mr. Darcy knows that I am overtired and wish to rest for this dance," I explained.

Giving me a look, Mr. Darcy whispered to me desperately.

"But you are not dancing?"

"Of course, I am not dancing. Why would I want to dance with anyone else but you?"

He gave me a sly smile.

"Woman, you are evil."

"Yes, that is the tone."

A little upset at me sitting out the set while obliging him to dance with Maria, he took her hand and he glared at me. I do believe that he was going to get his revenge on me, in one way or the other. Mary began to play, and the second set began. At first, I was thirsty, so I went over to the punch bowl and poured myself a glass. As I did so, I saw Colonel Fitzwilliam sitting down, due to having no more women to stand up with. It didn't affect him, for I saw that he was amidst a conversation with Mama, who was seated next to him.

"Oh, Colonel," she narrated animatedly, "if you were here, you would have seen it. The Netherfield Ball was the talk of the county, and indeed, there was nothing like it. And that is where the real surprise of it all is. After that ball, I knew that Jane and Mr. Bingley were madly in love with each other, so I was all ready to prepare for him to make my dear Jane an offer, and what do you think? All my plans and dreams were overturned, and the reverse had happened. He left Netherfield the next day, and eventually, my daughters return to me, and Elizabeth is the one who is engaged to Mr. Darcy! And I thought that they had despised each other. Sometimes we parents are the last to know what are in the hearts of their children."

"I can attest to that," Colonel Fitzwilliam agreed. "My eldest brother is often tossed in love and my parents never know the way in which the winds of his heart blows. Sometimes, we believe he is in love with one woman, then we are all in error. I suppose that I am no better, for they do not know where my heart lies either."

"But you appear to be a good man," she assured him, "so gentle and steady. And your brother is the eldest? Is he as kind as you are?"

Colonel Fitzwilliam's eyes became downcast.

"He and I are of two different temperaments. If you ask me of such because his being the eldest makes him more eligible, I will be truthful. I love my brother, but do not consider him as a suitable match for your daughters. His passions are not what they ought to be, and your daughters deserve better."

"Oh, you are so very good to care for them," she said, "and what my daughters did deserve was for my poor Mr. Bennet and I to have sons to protect them. But you know our situation. We are homeless, Colonel, and I have one duty now: protect my children and make sure that they have a home. The last thing that I wish is to see them destitute. That is why Elizabeth's attachment is the best thing in the world. By her being so, that will throw the rest of my children into the path of other rich men. Jane was supposed to save us with her match to Mr. Bingley. Indeed, I had set all my expectations on that score, initially. But I cannot help but still desire that match to be made. And Mr. Bingley, naturally, respects your advice. Can you please assure him that Jane still prefers him to any other man? It seems a crime that two people should be separate, when they are so attached to each other. And... this will help save my family. Could you, Colonel? I depend upon the kindness of men such as yourself."

This conversation produced a whole manner of sensations within me. The impropriety of it! First, Mama should never have appealed to him to influence Mr. Bingley's decision, but for her to make her aims evident to him, was too much! Yes, women often threw their children into the path of wealthier individuals, but to be so callous and cold about it... it hurt. And she did not know that she was causing the Colonel so much pain. I was certain that he wished to run away and hide from us all. Ignorant of the desires of his heart, Mama was showing him how his love for Jane would never be as desirable as Mr. Bingley's love for her.

Before the conversation would drive Colonel Fitzwilliam to distraction, the only option that I had was to try and save him from suffering any longer.

"Colonel and Mama," I said, walking up to them. "Are we not having a lovely evening?"

"Oh, it is the loveliest evening ever," Mama answered. "I am just so beside myself."

"Your joy has added a blush to your cheeks," I said, "and I have learned that I do not know my own mind. First, I feel tired, so I do not dance. And now I discover that I had wanted to dance the entire time."

"Well, I shall be happy to oblige you," Colonel Fitzwilliam offered, happy to remove himself from his present circumstance. Taking my hand, we joined the dancers and began.

"I have a secret," I said.

"And what is that?"

"Everyone in the town has discovered that they find you to be the worthiest of men."

He chuckled.

"Oh, do they?"

"Yes. So, I must warn your heart because they will try to steal it."

"I think that I am strong enough to learn forbearance, but never so proud that I cannot enjoy a compliment. If Hertfordshire has learned to like me, then I can admit to adoring them."

"An elegant arrangement, I am sure."

We continued to dance, where it was evident that I was trying to rally the spirits of a man whose spirits were wounded.

"So," Darcy said to me as we were ending the evening. As we prepared to go, he was wrapping my shawl around my shoulders. "First you say that you will not dance, and then I found you dancing."

"I was not as much dancing as I was trying to heal some wounds. My mother did something."

"What?"

I quickly told him what I had overheard.

He shook his head. "Oh, good lord. Your mama knew not the pain she was causing."

"No, she did not. I will talk to her when I get home, to advise her to exercise propriety when she speaks, but what of the poor Colonel?"

"I do not know if he would wish for me to address it, because we men can be very different than each other. When I am disturbed, I like talking about why I am, with people that I am intimate with. Other men do not like to speak about things. They only wish to confer with themselves."

"What sort of man is your cousin?"

"I don't know. I've never seen him heartbroken before."

"Oh."

Our carriage was brought round, and we left for home.

"I had so much fun," Lydia extoled. "I almost forgot about Brighton. Yes, I have."

"I confess that I did enjoy the evening as well," Mary admitted.

"You both sound alike," Kitty observed. "That may very well be the first time that this has ever happened."

Lydia and Mary groaned.

"And the last," I said, then I looked at Mama, who was talking animatedly with Jane.

What a woman! She knew not the pain that she had inflicted.

We arrived at Longbourn and quickly prepared to retire, for each of us were exhausted.

Due to being tired myself, I initially told myself that I didn't need to go to Mama, because I could always just wait tomorrow. However, I knew that if I didn't do it now, I might lose my nerve.

Therefore, I walked to Mama's room where we would have a difficult discussion over candlelight.

———

Knocking on her door, I asked if I could enter. When I did, I saw Hill waiting on her.

"Now, Hill," Mama said, "have you got it all right?"

"Yes, ma'am," Hill said, "tomorrow, you want to see if I can get duck, potato soup, rice, and a salad."

"If Mr. Darcy is to come, I want him to feel that he can eat as well here as in his own home."

"Very good, ma'am," Hill confirmed, and she smiled at me as she left.

"Are those foods that Mr. Darcy likes, Elizabeth?" Mama asked me.

"I do believe he will love it," I confirmed, closing the door.

"Oh, you come to speak to me."

"I do," I said, sitting down. "First, Mama, I wish for you to know and believe that I appreciate that you wish to make Mr. Darcy comfortable. And I do appreciate your concern for us. But I did accidentally overhear your discussion with Colonel Fitzwilliam this evening."

"That is a terrible habit, Elizabeth!" she reprimanded. "Listening on other people's conversations is wrong. How can you expect to be mistress of Pemberley and be so indelicate?"

"Me? Indelicate? How can you say so when that is how you often behave? Mama, you spoke about throwing my sisters into the path of rich men in front of the Colonel. That is avarice, inconsiderate, and indirectly slighting the poor Colonel for being a younger son."

"I will not apologize for wishing to give you all the best."

"I appreciate that."

"No, you don't!" she hissed, getting up. "You never have appreciated it. Do you know what it's like to get married, have five daughters, no sons, and you can't save them from losing the home they were raised in? Do you begin to understand how worthless that makes a mother feel?"

I was silenced for a moment.

"I am your mother," she continued, "my duty is to protect you from the evil ways of the world. From a young age, I learned that I could not do that, and it was never going to be. Therefore, what choice do I have now but marry you all off, to make sure you have a home, and are protected. Your father is dead, therefore, I do what I must."

"You don't see, do you?" I finally gathered. "I have *always* appreciated your desire to protect us, but it was your means through which you attempted to do it. You threw me at Mr. Collins, despite that you knew I could never be happy with him.

Do you know how it feels for your mother to try to force you into a match that would make you miserable for the rest of your life?"

"I didn't know your father very long when I married him."

"And look what happened? You both lost your love for each other. I don't want the life you had with him. I want a husband who loves me forever. I could have never had that with Mr. Collins. You knew this, but you didn't care. So, yes, I do appreciate your instincts to always protect us, but not when it leads to endangering us. And by speaking the way that you did this evening, without any shame or labelling us as crass fortune hunters, you made us look mercenary and expose us to the contempt of the world. That will hurt Kitty, Mary, and Lydia's chances. Jane will be fine, but their fates are more questionable. For I tell you this now, that men do not like being obviously sought after for their money. It hurts their sense of importance. Men are like us women; we want to be chosen because there is something in us all worth loving. Therefore, for you to make it evident that you are pushing us out into the world just for the sake of looking at men's purses and not their personalities, you lessen the chances of them making a match, rather than increasing it. Do you understand what I mean?"

Mama sat back down, disturbed.

"I…"

"And to tell you this truth," I said, "I ask you now to never utter it again. You spoke about Mr. Bingley's attachment to Jane, in front of the Colonel, and didn't know that you caused pain. Mama, Colonel Fitzwilliam is also in love with Jane."

"What?" Mama gasped.

"Yes. It happened when we were in London. Ignorant of Mr. Bingley's history with Jane, the dear Colonel fell in love with her. Jane decided not to choose either of them, for fear of hurting the other. That is why she is not married to Mr. Bingley. She did it out of concern for Colonel Fitzwilliam's heart."

"Oh, the poor boy. And I do like the Colonel, very much! If only he was born first."

"As you told him such, when asking about his older brother. I know that you didn't know that you were hurting him, but I tell you this now to show you what can happen when you do not moderate what you talk about. The Colonel is in pain now."

"Well," Mama said, "I shall make up for it. I will be very kind and agreeable whenever I see him again."

I sighed, relieved.

"That is good, Mama. And I am not mad at you, nor ungracious for your concern to protect us. Your intentions have always been very good. It is merely how you execute your intentions that I must question. I do love you, Mama, but please. Do this for me?"

"I… I don't know. I just don't know, Elizabeth. I am sad now."

"Very well," I said, "will you at least promise me to never talk about this again? This is not our secret to expose. Also, never ask Jane about either gentleman. She does not wish to talk of it. Please let that part of our lives take its natural course."

"I can do that," she replied eagerly. "I will do that."

I kissed her head and began to leave.

"Elizabeth?" she called to me.

"Yes?"

"Yes, you are correct that I knew you did not love Mr. Collins. And I encouraged the match without thinking or caring about how you would have felt about it. It was unfair to do, and the only thing that I can say, in defense of myself, is that I was scared. This was my chance to secure Longbourn and save us all. I couldn't help it."

"I know. But I wish that you had fought for me, rather than against me."

I bade her goodnight.

CHAPTER 14

THE ONLY SENSIBLE THING TO DO

The next day, Mr. Darcy did come with Mr. Bingley, Georgiana, and Elena. Since all were there, Mama was beside herself, but she did notice the absence of another.

"But what of the dear Colonel?" Mama inquired. "I was looking forward to seeing him again."

"Colonel Fitzwilliam expressly told us to give his apologies," Georgiana explained, "he told us this morning that he was too long away from his duties, and he had to return to his regiment."

"Oh, that is most unlucky. When you next write to him, please tell him that he was very much missed, and we long to see him again."

"Yes, I shall."

"Today is a rather fine day," Mr. Bingley said, "and I long to be out and about. Would anyone be willing to walk to Meryton after teatime?"

We all agreed to this, and after half an hour, we set out for town. As we walked, Mr. Darcy and I were close to each other, while separate from the others.

"I suppose that I owe you an explanation. Richard knew why you chose to dance. He told me to thank you for saving him from an unpleasant conversation."

"Oh," I sighed, relieved. "And I wished to not be so obvious that I had been doing that."

"He appreciated it."

Removing a letter from his jacket's pocket, he handed it to me.

"This is a letter for Jane," I said, reading the name on the front.

"It is. Richard wrote it last night and allowed me to read it. It was necessary."

"It is not proper for a gentleman to give a letter to a lady, but this must be important."

"It is. Believe me, it is something that Jane needs to see, for the sake of her moving on with her life. Elizabeth, promise me that you will give it to her. Yes, it is not proper, but sometimes, what is improper is also necessary."

"I shall."

After a few hours, we returned to Longbourn, where Mama rushed in, saying that Kitty had a letter from a publishing house.

"It's from Allen & Unwin Publishing House," Kitty said, "the place that I had sent my book to."

She looked around at us all. Since we were all present, we all were there to witness whether she was accepted or rejected.

"Perhaps you might wish to read your letter later," Jane offered.

"Yes," I added, "in case…"

"No," Kitty said, "if I have been rejected, then I ought to prepare myself. Writers rarely get approval from publishing houses when they first try. I knew the world that I was entering."

Exhaling, she opened the letter and began to read. As she perused the contents, her mouth dropped open and her eyes widened. The suspense was killing us.

A second rose.

A minute fell.

At last, Kitty lowered the letter.

"They accepted my book. They are going to publish my book!"

For a second, we were silent, then we all burst out in an uproar. Our congratulations became a chorus as we repeatedly issued our joy for her.

"My daughter is being published!" Mama cried, fluttering

about. "My daughter is being published! My daughter is being published! My daughter is…"

She passed out from the exertion of being exhilarated.

———

Fortunately, Mr. Bingley had been standing right next to her and caught her as she collapsed.

We rushed to her as he lowered her down onto the sofa and we began to fan her.

"Where are her smelling salts?" I asked.

"I've got it," Jane said, retrieving the salt and then placing it under Mama's nose. Eventually, she opened her eyes and woke up to see us staring down at her.

"I was not asleep," she rushed out.

"No, Mama," Lydia said, "you fainted."

"I fainted?"

"Yes," Mary said, "after you heard that Kitty is getting her book published."

"You are getting your book published!" Mama cried, taking Kitty's hand. "You are getting your book published!"

"Mother," Jane advised, "you must calm yourself, or you will get excited again."

"Because I am excited. Oh, congratulations, Kitty!"

"Thank you, Mama," Kitty said.

"And I had never thought that you were clever enough to write a whole novel, but you were the entire time."

Kitty rolled her eyes.

"Thank you, Mama," Kitty repeated, her tone dripping with sarcasm.

"This is truly a day of celebration!" Georgiana cried.

"Kitty, this is marvelous," Elena added.

"Thank you, and I cannot believe it, myself," Kitty said. "Writers don't get people to publish their books for years of repeated attempts and repeated failures. Mr. Darcy, I am not insensitive to the fact that the *only* reason I have gotten this offer is because you allowed me to use your name."

"His name?" Mama repeated.

"Yes. I was worried that no one would give me a chance, so I asked Mr. Darcy if I could write under a male pseudonym, using his last name. Also, the fact that I mailed my book from Rosings Park probably did add to its attraction. I told them to forward all mail here in case we were returned by then, and they have! There is the possibility that I got accepted on the connections that we have made, rather than the content of my book. I would not even believe my good fortune myself, if the letter had arrived with my book in it, but Allen & Unwin Publishing House still has it, therefore, it is safe to say this is genuine. Mr. Darcy, I cannot thank you enough."

"It was my pleasure."

"Now, the only thing to do is to gather the courage to tell them that I am not who I said that I was."

"Would it help if I wrote a letter explaining it?" Mr. Darcy asked. "If I do, then they will not take it amiss."

"Oh, yes, please," Kitty replied, eagerly. "I will love you forever if you do that, Mr. Darcy. They will be too impressed by you to care at all that I had embellished everything."

"I'll write the letter now and have it sent so that it can reach London quickly. Mrs. Bennet, might I trouble you for a pen, ink, and paper?"

"Yes, you can indeed!" Mama called. "Hill, please bring us some pen and paper for Mr. Darcy to send a letter."

Mr. Darcy sat down, composed the letter as we all praised Kitty for her triumph. With this new bit of news, the rest of the day was spent occupied with discussions on her next novel.

"Sadly, the only reason they would accept my next book is if the first book sells successfully," Kitty acknowledged, "and I have to face that possibility."

"You are so inclined to think the worst, Kitty," Elena pointed out. "That is ungenerous to yourself."

"It is," Kitty said, taking her hand, "but I have to confront this now, so as not to get overconfident later. I love my books. They are like my children. However, not all children become popular. Therefore, it is best to embrace the truth now, in case I need to prepare myself later. Also, I was all aglow about writing another novel. This one was about two stepsisters who become very good friends, and both find themselves in love with the same man."

"That would be rich," Lydia said, "but it has been known to happen."

"Yes. I named it 'Wives & Daughters', but I quickly abandoned the idea."

"Why?" Georgiana asked.

"I don't know." Kitty squinted, looking ahead at an invisible horizon. "But the story has a familiar feeling, as if I have the suspicion that it has been written by someone else. But I have other ideas, and I just have to meld them into some defined shape."

"My sister is a writer," Lydia exclaimed. "What a good joke!"

"A joke implies that something is not real," Mary corrected. "Kitty's writing is true."

"Well," Mr. Bingley said, "I have thought of your writing, and I have a few good stories that I am not afraid of sharing."

"I like stories," Kitty said, "stories help give characters a history. And the more history that a character has before the book begins, makes the story you write about them feel more real. Go on, Mr. Bingley, I am ready for anything!"

"Well," Elena said, "be sure to write the story of a woman whose family cast her out because she didn't marry as they wished, but the marriage never came to fruition."

"Yes, I admit that I was already going to use that. It is too good a tale to not use."

"I am flattered," Elena said with a laugh.

"Mr. Darcy," Kitty said, "do not put away the rest of the paper and ink that you were given. I believe that I will need to use it to help me remember everything that I am told this day."

Eagerly, everyone began to offer stories from their past and Mama spent the day making sure that everyone was properly tended to. Other than that, it was one of the easiest and carefree visits ever.

After a few hours, the Netherfield party had to depart, with another invitation for us to join them tomorrow for lunch.

When we were all finished dressing for bed, I went to Jane's door and finally gave her the letter.

"Who is this letter from?" Jane asked.

"Colonel Fitzwilliam."

"For a man to send me a letter!"

"Jane, he had no choice. According to Mr. Darcy, the letter is necessary. Therefore, I urge you to read it, and forgive the Colonel for breaching protocol."

Jane took the letter, and I began to leave.

"No, don't leave, Lizzy. After reading it, I am sure that I will want to talk of its contents."

Jane sat at her desk while I waited. When she finished, she placed the letter next to the candle.

"He has revoked his proposal of marriage," Jane explained. "The Colonel has removed his affections and wishes me well in finding happiness elsewhere. He wishes for God to bless me and give me everything that he thinks is my worth. He wants me to feel entirely free to live my life as I choose."

"Oh, Jane, I…"

She lowered the letter over the candle, where the fire began to burn it.

"What are you doing!" I asked.

"Protecting him from being discovered of sending a letter to a lady." She walked to the fireplace and put it over the coals. "I do not want anything terrible to be said of him."

"I know the reason that he did this," I explained, "and it wasn't due to losing his affections for you. I am sure that he still felt it all. I firmly believe that he did it when he discovered that Mama still dreams about you marrying a rich man."

"How do you know that? Did she say anything directly malicious towards him?"

"Not intentionally. I overheard her talking to him once. You know how she talks. She simply commented on my engagement to Mr. Darcy, and how she was happy that the connection would introduce my sisters to other rich men. Colonel Fitzwilliam could not help but be affected by this and wish for you to have the life that he could not give. In a prudential light, this was the only sensible thing to do."

"I am sorry. I wish that she had not hurt him so. While I do not deny that I am happy to not be in the middle of two worthy men, I still feel attached to his happiness, and wish that he never feels pain over me."

"But you are happier now, aren't you?" I realized. "To be torn between two men like that is hard, because you cannot choose either of them."

"And I was not worthy of either of them to begin with. But for both men to be so inconvenienced by the other, over me, was never what I wanted. Now the decision has been made for me, and I am very happy over it. Colonel Fitzwilliam deserves an heiress. May he find it, and may he be happy. And I cannot feel any regret for my love for Mr. Bingley. Of course, Mr. Bingley might never choose me again."

"He will. I have the feeling that Mr. Darcy will tell him about Colonel Fitzwilliam's choice. Therefore, I do not believe that this is a matter of 'will Mr. Bingley propose to you, but 'when'."

"Yes. It all has to do with a matter of time."

"I do believe that time will be kind."

"I hope so. It would be nice to have her as a friend. Until then, we have the future Mrs. Darcy and a writer in our family. Fate has been very good to us, so I can forgive if it is not kind toward me. No family can have everything."

I looked at the fireplace, at the cinders that the letter had burned into.

"All of those months of indecision, inner disquiet, and tension," I observed, "and it all ends merely with a letter being written and burned."

"So much that ends in so little a way."

"Perhaps, there is nothing more fitting than that, and it is how it should be."

I kissed her cheek and bade her goodnight.

When I passed Mary's room, I saw her sitting in her rocking chair and looking up at the moon.

"I'm surprised that you are not reading in bed," I observed.

"No, I am not," Mary said, still looking out of the window.

"What is so fascinating about the night sky?" I asked.

"There is always something fascinating about the sky, be it day or night. There is something about it that makes a person feel as if there is much more to life… if we just find it."

"I know what you are feeling," I theorized.

"You do?"

"Yes. You are wondering, throughout all of this, where does your road lead?"

"Yes."

"The only thing that I can suggest is not to look for a forced path. Often, it has a way of finding us. Just be open to whatever may come."

I bade her goodnight and went to my room.

CHAPTER 15

A PROPOSAL WORTH THE WAIT

The next day, we did go to Netherfield and dine there, and I observed Mr. Bingley very closely. It was evident that he felt more public in occupying Jane's company and keeping her to himself.

"You told him, didn't you?" I asked Mr. Darcy.

"Yes, I thought it best to do so. Jane has been forced into waiting long enough for them to decide the best course of action."

"Yes, I agree. She has waited long enough."

When the lunch was over, we sat down and played cards. Darcy and I were placed at the same table as Bingley and Jane. He and I might as well had not been there at all, because Jane and Bingley spoke mostly to each other, only sparing a moment for us whenever they had to place a card down. It was such at the Netherfield Ball, where both were so wrapped up in each other's company, that both could barely have any time to attend to anyone else but each other.

When it came time for us to depart, I voiced my findings to Mr. Darcy.

"After all that has happened," I announced, "between the machinations of the Bingley sisters, yourself, Colonel Fitzwilliam, and a plethora of elopements later, everything is ending where it properly was supposed to. They are united again. Darcy, I shall kick you if you do not tell me that I was right."

"Sadly, I have no choice but to admit that contrary to all my previous attempts to separate them both, you were right in the end."

"It was fate. You see, you men are left to wonder at the cosmos and the great questions of life. That leaves us women so much time to see the truth of grand triviality."

We departed and Mama couldn't help herself as she became verbose on predicting that Mr. Bingley was paying close attention to Jane again. For if she were to have a daughter at Pemberley, to have another one at Netherfield would make her eternally happy.

Jane was in the best of looks, for the burden of two men's affections was lifted from her shoulders. Therefore, the glow to her cheeks was enhanced and she felt that she could bestow her powers of pleasing without betraying anyone.

I dared not ask her about what she was feeling, but it was no matter. Kitty would use this all to make something else up, and her imagination was enough to fill the void of what the truth really was.

The next day, only Mr. Darcy and Mr. Bingley came to Longbourn.

When seeing only them, explanations were quickly given to excuse Georgiana's and Elena's absence. Elena needed the day to write letters to her family and friends back in her home county, to establish a connection again. Georgiana found that she woke up with a headache, and just wished to spend the day in bed, in solitude.

"I am sorry for Georgiana's health," I said, "I hope that she is given a cold compress. That may help."

"She is being very well attended to, I promise," Darcy explained, "or I would not have felt comfortable in leaving her."

"You came upon us right when we were about to pick flowers," Jane said, explaining the aprons that we had not had time to remove.

"Oh, we do not need to hinder your progress," Mr. Bingley said, "Darcy, would you be willing to escort the ladies as they pick flowers?"

"I think it a lovely image to witness."

"As do I."

Joined by Darcy and Bingley, Jane and I set out. Both men offered to hold our baskets and new flower bulbs as we went to the gardens. Jane sat down on the ground and began to plant the bulbs and I thought to be generous.

"While you both plant the bulbs," I said, "Darcy will escort me as I pick the flowers on the other side of the garden. Is that agreeable?"

"Yes," Jane said, "I will be able to plant these myself."

"And if the duty gets too strenuous," Mr. Bingley said, removing his jacket and rolling up his sleeves, "I do not fear having dirty knees and hands by toiling in dirt."

"When I was a child, I was notorious for making mud pies," Jane told him as they began to plant together.

"I did as well. A proper childhood should always include getting dirty from time to time."

"I believe so as well. That is what soap and water are for. To wipe away the evidence."

He laughed and soon we lost sight of them as we disappeared around the house. I began to pick flowers and place them in his basket.

"You are giving them time alone," Darcy observed.

"As repayment for all the times that Jane looked for spiders in our hotel room," I replied, giving him an arched look. "I had to show my gratitude in any way that I can."

"Jane looks happy."

"She is. I know that she feels a little guilty for inviting Bingley's attentions so soon after the Colonel removed his, but I do not believe she will let that stop her from choosing joy for herself."

"And she ought not to. Richard does need to marry, with consideration of a woman's income, sadly. He deserves better, but that is the fate of a second son. He will regret Jane, but over time, he will regard this moment as a bit of enchantment passing through his heart and warming him for a while."

"Men like Colonel Fitzwilliam never have to worry about

securing a woman's heart. He is like you; there are more women in love with him than he knows what to do with."

"That cannot be true," he professed, his eyes twinkling, despite himself.

"Oh, but it is. And you know it. I daresay that the only reason that I managed to win you was because I was so different than the many women who wanted to win your heart. In fact, I believe that if you had not decidedly disliked the people of Hertfordshire when you first came here, all my sisters would have fallen in love with you. I was merely the fortunate one to find my way into your affections."

"You are flattering me so much that I might get a swelled head over it."

"I will find something to insult you about later. That way your head shall keep its ideal shape. I could not marry a man whose head was on the verge of exploding."

He smiled as I picked another flower.

After half an hour, we could not stall any longer, therefore we walked around the house to join them both. After all, Jane and I had to take the flowers and dry them. When we went to meet them, we found Jane and Mr. Bingley holding hands and gazing into each other's eyes.

When they saw us, they instinctively moved away from each other.

"Forgive us," I said, turning around to leave, when Jane raised her hand.

"No, do not go, Elizabeth," Jane said, her cheeks red from blushing.

"Yes, Darcy, do not go," Bingley responded. He whispered something in Jane's ear, she nodded, he stood up, dusted off his knees, looked bashful, and amused. "This is not the manner which I wished to face your mother. Looking like I fell into a ditch. Darcy, please, it would mean a great deal if you could join me."

"Of course."

Together, both men entered the house and I looked at Jane as she stood up.

"Well?" I asked.

Her face was all alight as her feelings poured forth.

"Oh, Lizzy!" she cried, opening her arms, and rushing to me. Closing my arms around her, we embraced, and words were not spoken.

"Tell me that I am to be happy for you," I pleaded, "tell me that I may be happy for you at last!"

"You can and you may," she cried. "He loves me, Lizzy. After all this time, he still loves me. He apologized for allowing himself to be persuaded against me initially."

"Well, he discovered his own will, in the end. That is enough."

"It is. A part of me feels terrible for choosing Mr. Bingley so soon after Colonel Fitzwilliam's rejection, but I cannot stop myself."

"It is right to. But Colonel Fitzwilliam did so to free you, to let your heart find its true path. Do not question it or doubt it. You have found love, Jane, and the love has been returned to you. Do not question it! Do not doubt it! Just chase it."

"We are to be married, and I am the happiest woman in the world. Why can't everyone be as happy as me? All deserve it."

"*Some* deserve it. And others deserve their Wickhams. And others deserve their Mr. Collinses. But those who deserve their Bingleys, yes, I do quite agree with you."

We heard our mother's cries from within.

"And now Mama knows of it." We looked at each other. "Now she may faint again."

When we did enter at last, Mama was beside herself and could not sit still for a moment. And when she came upon the happiest plan of all, she reached a new plateau of exhilaration.

"A double wedding!" she cried. "Elizabeth and Jane, you ought to marry together! Mr. Darcy and Mr. Bingley, what do you think?

A double wedding at Pemberley church? Oh, please! It would make me the happiest creature in the world."

"I find it to be a splendid idea!" Bingley observed.

"I find it to be agreeable as well," Darcy confirmed.

"Then it is settled," she cried. "You both are to be the happiest couples in the world!"

"The happiest couples in the world," I repeated. "I am inclined to believe it."

News spread over Hertfordshire very quickly, and we Bennets went from being regarded as being the most fortunate family in Hertfordshire, to being the most fortunate family in England.

"Two daughters married to two of the grandest men ever," Lady Lucas observed, "and to think, all of that happened right here in Longbourn."

I often marvel at how quickly everything can come together. After many visits from our neighbors, wishing us their congratulations, all of us Bennets had to quit Longbourn to journey to Pemberley.

"Oh, I shall see Pemberley," Mama cried. "I have been told that it is the best place in the world."

"There shall be room for you all," Darcy informed us, "and if you forgive me, but I also invited the Gardiners. I hope that I was not being presumptuous."

"Not at all," I assured him, "for I believe there could be no better arrangement."

"The Colonel will also be present as well as Mr. Bingley's family. Hopefully, everything shall go smoothly."

"One can only dream. I do believe that all the elopements are behind us. But what of the Colonel? Will this wedding hurt him?"

"It will. But Richard has survived greater obstacles than heartbreak. He has learned to live despite the pain of it. Also, with his sudden departure from Netherfield, he needed time to himself and to throw himself into his work. He will have been given a month by the time we get married. If he has not had time to reign his heart in by then, then I have given him permission not to come."

"We have to be prepared if he doesn't know how to recover in time. Either way, I believe in him."

It is remarkable how quickly everything was arranged.

Soon, all Longbourn and Netherfield Park occupants were on the road, and heading North for Pemberley, early in the morning.

After a long and arduous journey, we finally arrived at Derbyshire.

"When will we reach Pemberley?" I asked Georgiana, as we turned down a lane.

"You are already in it," Georgiana remarked.

"We are?" Kitty asked. "But where is the house?"

"Oh, it will be a little while before you see it."

"Well, the estate around it is very beautiful," I said, amazed. "And I confess that I never knew that the grounds were this extensive."

"Yes, indeed it is." Mary gasped, her face looking out of the window alongside the rest of us. "This is remarkable."

We continued to drive through grounds more, and still the house was not produced.

"Georgiana," I asked, "precisely how much land does your brother own?"

"Roughly ten miles."

We all blinked, shocked by this.

"Ten miles?" Jane echoed. "Are you in earnest?"

"Very much so," Georgiana laughed, amazed at our astonishment. "We live in a secluded world."

"I confess that I never knew it was this large," I professed. "Who is the man that I am engaged to?"

"Soon, we are about to see the house as the trees clear," Georgiana directed, "on the left. Wait for it."

Soon, the trees cleared away and we gazed upon our first sight of Pemberley.

"Oh, my word!" Mama wailed.

"There it is," Lydia said, "my word, it is the biggest house that I have ever seen!"

"It is wonderful," Kitty said, "now that is the place to help be a muse for me."

"How do you like the house, Lizzy?" Georgiana asked.

"I...I...I will be mistress of that?" I asked.

"Yes."

"I cannot believe that—it is the most beautiful home I have ever seen. Indeed, I have never seen a place so happily situated. I love it very much, indeed. But what if I am not a good enough mistress for it? Never mind, that is nonsense. I will make sure that my courage will see me through."

"Oh, you better do so!" Mama said. "You must not let Mr. Darcy down at all."

"Mama, Elizabeth will not do that," Jane assured me. "You know that she will not."

"All that I know is that a time like this, a mother is needed more than ever. On the eve of getting married, a woman feels all sorts of things that a mother understands."

"Like what?" Kitty asked.

"Like inward contempt of the man that you are about to marry."

"What?" I nearly recoiled.

"It is but a trifle. Often, right before the ceremony takes place, a woman can sometimes have a fleeting hatred for the man she is about to become wife to. It is strange, but there it is." Mama pat my knee. "I will be here for you, when that time comes."

"Mama, that is very good of you," I replied, sarcastically.

"I know dear, I know."

Ignoring her, I looked out at Pemberley as we drew nearer to it.

As we neared the estate, all the servants were lined up outside of it, with one woman at the head.

"Georgiana," I asked, "is that the housekeeper?"

"Yes. Her name is Mrs. Reynolds. She is the best housekeeper in the world. You will love her."

"Is she the sort to know all of Mr. Darcy's likes and dislikes?"

"She knows it all. From his favorite dish to his daily habits."

"Good. Georgiana, do me the wonderful favor of being mistress at Pemberley for the first few weeks. It would be better if I watched your habits and then improved myself on my own."

"That will not do, dear," Mama stressed. "Of course, this is spoken out of no disrespect for you, Miss Darcy, but worry over my daughter. If Mr. Darcy sees you as not fulfilling your duties as mistress, he will worry that you will disappoint him. I do not want him thinking negatively of you. A woman ought to take control of her house as soon as it is hers. That indicates leadership."

"Sound advice, but there was a woman here before I was. Georgiana was mistress of Pemberley before I take up the title. For me to supplant her soon after arrival might be forceful. Besides, wouldn't Mr. Darcy prefer it if I respect his sister's feelings?"

"Oh," Mama said, "yes, that is a better idea than mine, I do not deny. A woman ought to look like a dutiful mistress, but there is something to be said for considering other's feelings. Very well, Elizabeth, I declare that you are correct. Yes, I believe that Mr. Darcy will like that."

I glanced at Georgiana, who bit back a smile.

Our carriages reached the house and Mrs. Reynolds stepped forward as we disembarked.

"Mrs. Reynolds," Georgiana said merrily. "We said that we would bring a large party to visit, and we have."

"Yes, I see the number of you, and this will be a delightful challenge," the old woman noted as Mr. Darcy approached her.

"Mrs. Reynolds, I am certain that you have done an exquisite duty of preparing everything. And I have brought you a fair mistress. Mrs. Reynolds, this is my fiancée, Miss Elizabeth Bennet."

"Mrs. Reynolds," I voiced, merrily, "it is a pleasure to meet you."

"And we are all very happy to make your acquaintance as well," she responded. "Never did I think any woman was good enough for my master, but I believe that I stand corrected."

"Oh, no, that will not do," I corrected her. "I thank you for believing in me, but we shall know if I am good enough for him in time. However, I promise, I shall try to live up to the epitaph that you have placed on me. Might I introduce you to all my family?"

"Of course."

"This is my mother, Mrs. Bennet. My sisters, Miss Jane Bennet, Miss Mary, Miss Kitty, and Miss Lydia. And while she is not my family yet, this is Miss Elena Darcy."

"Miss Elena Darcy?" Mrs. Reynolds said. "Another member of the Darcy family that I have never met?"

"Through no fault of my own, I assure you," Elena said. "I am the late Mr. Darcy's niece. My father was your late master's brother, and they have been estranged for years."

Mrs. Reynolds pressed a hand to her chest. "Oh, good lord."

"Estrangement is something my father does very well. He makes a talent of it."

"Also, Mrs. Reynolds, there is some very good news to add to my happy day," Darcy continued. "Mr. Bingley is engaged to my fiancée's sister, Miss Jane Bennet, and we shall have a double wedding here."

Mrs. Reynolds turned a whiter shade of pale.

"A double wedding," she extoled, "a double wedding!"

"Yes," Mama said, "exciting, isn't it?"

"Yes, it is indeed!" Mrs. Reynolds matched her excitement and clapped. "A double wedding! Oh, this is the most delightful news and will be the social event of the county! Congratulations, Mr. Bingley! And to you as well, Miss Bennet."

"You are all kindness and goodness, ma'am," Mr. Bingley responded, "as always."

Before we entered, I turned to all the servants.

"Darcy, all these people work under us?" I asked.

"Yes, they do."

Smiling to them, I curtsied.

The men bowed and the women curtsied in return.

"I hope they will like me."

"They will love you."

We all entered as our luggage was brought in and tea and cakes were already waiting for us.

The refreshment assortment was elegant and there was fruit alongside the cakes and biscuits.

"Fruit with tea," Mama exclaimed as she ate from her plate. "How delightful. I wish that I had thought of such. When I return to Longbourn, I will always have fruit for visitors with the other assortment."

"It is something only Mrs. Reynolds thinks of," Georgiana boasted.

"You sound ingenious, Mrs. Reynolds," I said.

"I wish to make my masters happy," Mrs. Reynolds replied. "I only hope I do the right thing. But for all of you here, well, this will be quite the treat."

"And there may be more of us on the wedding day," Georgiana pointed out.

"Yes, we will have more guests," Darcy added. "I wrote to Mrs. Reynolds, preparing her for more of us to come."

"It is not just that," Georgiana said, "but of something that I was considering when traveling here."

"You look aglow with a scheme on your mind, Georgiana?" Kitty guessed, amused.

"Sometimes being properly social can be tiresome, but what is proper to do must be done. There are other great houses in the county, from Matlock and Blenheim, to Chatsworth and Warwick. These families have invited us to their social events, but we never invite them to any."

"Because I never give any," Darcy responded, which led to everyone laughing. This surprised Darcy, for he did not mean for it to be a joke in any way but was very serious.

"Correct," Georgiana said, "but if I am to show Elizabeth how to be mistress, then I have to develop my own skills. If we continue to accept their invitations, but we never invite them, perhaps we are not presenting ourselves as the best neighbors. What I mean is that this wedding can be the perfect excuse to invite them all for a ball here."

"A ball on our wedding?" I asked.

"The day after," Georgiana said. "For I can empathize, realizing that the last thing you would wish to do is be around other people after you get married."

"You understand me well," I said, "if Mr. Darcy wishes it, then I will agree."

Instinctively, everyone turned to Darcy.

"Unbelievable," he grunted. "I am placed in the difficult position of doing something that I do not wish to do. At all."

We still kept looking at him.

"And this will be the last time that I am forced into doing something that I do not wish to do."

We all breathed a sigh of relief.

Georgiana was correct. The best way for me to make myself agreeable to my neighbors as the new mistress of Pemberley was to make everyone feel as if I wished to know them.

Therefore, Pemberley had a double wedding to look forward to, then a ball the next evening.

Mrs. Reynolds had us shown to all our rooms, and she personally escorted me to my guestroom. On the day that I married Mr. Darcy, would I be given the mistress's bedroom.

"A beautiful room!" I declared, moving all around it. "So, this is where I will spend the happiest days of my life."

"Yes, indeed. You must be very excited."

"I am. Though I know that we place a lot of trouble on you. First you must prepare for the whole bridal party to come here after I marry, then you will have to prepare for a ball."

"Oh, I am excited. I have been trained for events such as this, and this will give me something to do. I have not hosted a ball here in years, so this will feel like the most exhilarating trial."

"Mrs. Reynolds, I must warn you about something."

"Yes?"

"I just realized how ominous I sound."

"I am prepared."

"It is nothing so very frightening, but only mildly frightening. My sister Jane is an ideal guest, and you will love her. Kitty is an inspiring writer, who can be rambunctious at times, but overall is pleasant and she also will not give you any trouble. Mary will be happy once she finds out where the music room and library are. She loves her studies and his very serious. But Kitty and Mary will, on occasion, say things that are more sincere than refined. Yet, my mother and youngest sister, Lydia, are very…"

"Spirited?" she finished my sentence. "Verbose, voluble, and a little impertinent?"

"Well, I cannot deny that you are correct there."

"Never fear, Miss Bennet. Whether silent or loud, mothers are mothers, and I am used to handling all sorts of them. I have had to tend to quite a few great ladies of the ton when they visited. So, I am accustomed to working under mothers who have demanding natures. As for your younger sisters, they are young. Kitty and Lydia appear to not even be twenty years old."

"They are not."

"Oh, then they are still developing their characters and it is not their fault. I have three daughters myself and they behaved in the same way when they were young."

"You have three daughters?"

"Yes. They do not work here, but one works at Blenheim as a governess and the other two are married and live in Hammersmith and Yorkshire."

"I am certain that they are lovely girls."

"They grew into that, yes, and I was strict with them when they were young, but that never kept me from understanding the behavior of children in their teenage years. Mark my words, Lydia and Kitty are nothing I have not seen before, and I will reserve judgement."

"Thank you," I replied. "And can you make certain to ask Kitty if she needs more paper and ink every now and again, for she needs more than the rest of us."

"Yes.

"One last thing, Mrs. Reynolds."

"Yes, dear?"

"I have spoken with Georgiana, and she has agreed to maintain the duties as mistress of Pemberley after I am married."

"You do not wish to occupy the role immediately?"

"No, I do not. I can assure you that it is not because I am lax, but I prefer to exercise things in moderation. She is mistress and you are the housekeeper. It has been this way for years. Therefore, for me to come in and reign over both those positions soon after entering the house will be disorientating for everyone. I will first observe you and Miss Darcy, learn what is the best way to run Pemberley, and will take up my duties when I am fully ready… or when Georgiana wishes to leave and visit friends. Whichever one comes first."

She gave me a warm smile. "That is a very wise sort of thing."

"Also, if you could write me a list of things that Mr. Darcy likes and dislikes, that would be best."

"I already have."

I started.

"Forgive me for anticipating you."

"It did give me a fright, but in a good way."

CHAPTER 16

LOVE & LOSS AT A WEDDING

The day for our double wedding came quickly, and I preferred it that way. The day before our happy event, there was a series of good news, followed by two good letters.

Colonel Fitzwilliam arrived in the morning, assuring us that his family was going to travel down from Matlock on the day of our wedding and then ride back home.

Aunt and Uncle Gardiner arrived in the afternoon, amazed at being able to stay at Pemberley.

And Sir Aleck Granger arrived in the evening, an hour before dinner time.

"Pemberley, are you real, or are you a mirage?" he exclaimed as he arrived. "Oh, what am I saying? Most of life *is* a mirage."

When seeing Elena, he began to bestow his powers of pleasing without care of being ridiculed for it.

Whatever worries that I had for Colonel Fitzwilliam's attitude when seeing Jane engaged to Mr. Bingley, I did not need to have. This was the first time that he saw them both after he sacrificed his own happiness by giving Jane up. His eyes were a little downcast, and he could not rally his spirits to be charming in their company very well, but he was still kind. Whatever he was feeling, he kept it to himself very well. Happy to find an outlet for his thwarted feelings, he sought solace in Kitty's company, and it worked. Whether because she was writing about soldiers, or because she always enjoyed his company, Kitty was eager to hear stories about Colonel Fitzwilliam's duties to his regiment and what his soldiers were like. Happy to have an occupation of some kind, he remained close to her.

As for Mama, despite her crass nature, she was, in all essentials, a *quintessential* mother. That was something that Elena and Georgiana did not have, therefore, both young women found pleasure in hearing her constantly talk about us, and when Sir Aleck arrived, Mama was even more flattered that such a distinguished man found her to be engaging. Sir Aleck was the perfect sort of aristocrat. He had all the money in the world to be independent, but he was born with a nature that accepted the follies of others, and the liberality of another person's mind. Also, he loved women's company. Ergo, when he was so welcome among that trio—and eventually joined by Lydia, all was perfect. The Gardiners were occupied with learning the particulars of Jane and Bingley finally coming to an arrangement and there was much lively discussion the evening before I married.

And this was all before the two good letters were read.

The first letter proved to be from Elena's parents—or rather from her mother. When seeing it, Elena was filled with trepidation, then she excused herself and read it by a window.

When she finished, she pocketed the letter and re-joined our party, looking a little red in the cheeks. The second letter was for Kitty, from Allen & Unwin Publishing house.

"Well," she said, "it's not my book mailed back to me, so we can hope that they are still willing to go through with it." She opened the letter and read it. When she finished, she was merry. "It is the most delightful thing in the world. Mr. Darcy, your letter did the trick! They are not upset with me at all, since I am still your sister-in-law, and they will still let me publish my novel under the pseudonym: A Lady."

"But totally unknown?" Aunt Gardiner asked. "Is that what you want?"

"The last thing I need is for people to think all my ideas are inspired by adventures here at Pemberley. Of course, I did read my first pages at the ball in Brighton, but hardly anyone would be willing to remember much of it. And even if they do, they perhaps never remembered my name, and they would probably never even read my books. Perhaps no one would. Can I persuade you all to buy a copy when it comes out?"

"Of course, we shall," Uncle Gardiner demanded, "and, I may buy two copies... and force one of our acquaintances to read it."

"But Kitty," Mama argued, "men do not wish to marry writers. I still am delighted for you, but I am not certain that you shall follow through with this."

"But I have no one considering me at all," Kitty returned, "and if I spent my life not doing things to appease a non-existent husband, then I would not be able to do anything."

"I just realized a sad truth; men do not want wives who write."

"Mama," I rebuked. "That is not fair."

"And forgive me, madam, but I resent the generality that you place on all us men," Colonel Fitzwilliam corrected "Not all of us men are the same."

"True," Sir Aleck supported, "some of us men commit the atrocious habit of not being afraid to be different. Shocking, I know! But so it is, Mrs. Bennet, that we men can be like you women...we are not all the same and therefore do not all fit a certain measuring system."

"Oh, but not all men are like you, Sir Aleck, Mr. Bingley, the Colonel, and Mr. Darcy, and the men in my family," Mama continued, "they want a specific type of woman."

"You did not see Sir Aleck and the Colonel's meaning, sister," Mr. Gardiner said, "and your words have proven theirs. You confirmed that not all of us men are the same."

"And that I ought to be the same as all women," Kitty continued. "You want me to adhere to a general rule of how we women ought to be, to adhere to a general rule of what men want. But when it comes to both sexes, making such sweeping generalizations are not real. There is not one and only *rule* and *regulation*."

"Oh, I wish you would not contradict me so," Mama said, "you have begun to question things too much. That is another quality that a man does not want in a wife."

"You argued with Father very often."

"You did, I saw that too," Lydia supported.

"I saw it as well," Mary confirmed.

"I cannot help but agree," I added.

Jane could not help but say nothing.

"Oh, my poor nerves, now you are all against me."

"They are not against you," Jane said, "but merely point out that your advice is different than your behavior."

"And I thought you were happy for me?" Kitty asked.

"I was, but I have quite changed my mind. And if this is how you all treat your mother, then I do not know what to say, but that you take delight in vexing me, as your father did. But Kitty, mark my words."

"You may consider them marked, but I have come too far. And if you were correct, that men do not want a woman like me just because I write, then I shall accept that I will never marry."

"Kitty, that is nonsense."

"Not at all, but practical. You tell me that men shall not choose me, just because I write. Well, I write, so no man will choose me. You have presented a reality with certain parameters in it, and so I adhere to them."

"If you don't publish, then you can save yourself."

"If I don't write, then I will have destroyed myself."

"I believe that Kitty will be well, book published or not," I finalized.

"I agree," Aunt Gardiner said, "she publishes it anonymously enough, therefore what harm is being done? None at all."

"Oh, that is true," Mama relented. "Yes, it makes sense when you put it like that. Very well, Kitty, you may publish... as long as you make sure that no one ever learns that it is you, and never mention your books to anyone."

"Forgive me," Kitty pressed, "but if someone asks me if I wrote my book, I will always tell the truth."

"You are now trying to spite me."

"No, I am just trying to complete myself."

"I will read her book," Sir Aleck announced. "Mrs. Bennet, if a knight reads your daughter's book, then clearly she has the right to sign my book."

"Oh," Mrs. Bennet said, her eyes fluttering from receiving his attentions, "yes, of course. I am proud of Kitty, as you know. I just cannot help but worry. I worry about you, my dear."

"I know," Kitty said, "but I know what I am doing. Mr. Unwin wishes for me to come to the publishing house when I arrive back in town—as soon as may be."

"To sign contracts?" Uncle Gardiner asked.

"Yes. I confess that I do not wish to be alone at that time. I feel it best for someone to be with me, for the sake of making sure that I am not being hoodwinked. Uncle and Aunt Gardiner, can I return to town with you after the wedding?"

"Yes, you may," Uncle Gardiner said, "and I shall accompany you, if we can set a date with Unwin."

"Thank you!"

"I can help escort you as well, Miss Kitty," Colonel Fitzwilliam offered. "I return to London after the wedding also, for the annual recruitment for the army."

"Really?" Kitty said. "That is splendid."

"Good. Swindlers have a habit of losing their courage when they are in the presence of a redcoat."

"And that's why I always loved a redcoat."

"I shall make sure to wear it well."

"Oh," Mama whined, "if only all men were like the men here. The world would be an easier place to get good husbands."

Eventually, we all retired to our rooms for bed, and I found myself still alive and awake. Jane and I had talked for quite some time in my bedroom when I heard a knock on the door.

"Come in," I said. The door opened and Mama came rushing in.

"I came to speak with you both about tomorrow and what to expect on your wedding night."

Jane and I gave each other an apprehensive look.

"Mama, we understand," I offered, "and you don't have to explain it to us if it causes you discomfort."

"Oh, no, a mother ought to do such things. First, Jane and Elizabeth, you have obtained the best matches in England. Jane, I knew that you would make a good match, but Elizabeth, it was such a shock."

I rolled my eyes.

"And that is what brings me to my first revelation," Mama said. "Perhaps I never took the pains to know that you were a different sort of woman, and that it was not wrong. Therefore, let me say that I am sorry for not seeing that you were so very special."

"Mother," I voiced, speechless. I had never thought that she would have said anything so kind to me before.

"And then there is Kitty, who I did not fully nurture in the manner that I knew how. You all must believe that I always did mean well with the advice I gave you all."

"We know, Mama," Jane assured her, "we know that you gave us all your effort and trials."

"But therein is my first message. First, being married and having children is not something that I can prepare you both for, because not all marriages are the same. I see that now. Just remember that you will make mistakes, and that is natural. But you make mistakes because you care, and there is no book to tell you how to be a parent. Much of it is instinct to protect your child. And with your husband, yes, it is also complicated."

She dabbed at her nose with a lace hanky. "I did argue with your father, and you perhaps may argue with yours. I cannot stop that from happening because it is inevitable. Yet, what I can advise is for you to not let any arguments make you out of spirits for long. Be angry, sad, or heartbroken, but always show him that you are willing to move on from that disagreement. Give him another chance. Implacable resentment is a cold triumph when its reward is that it caused a permanent separation between your husband and yourself. I remember the time that I did that, where I let my anger make me angry at your father for weeks. When I finally recovered from my resentment, it was too late. His love for me had sunk into indifference and we had never been able to find our way back to the people we were when we married."

"You never told us this," I said, touched that she would reveal it. "I wish that you had told us this long ago."

"Yes, well… I was very embarrassed by it. It is not easy when the blame for your marriage becoming loveless is mostly your fault. And lastly, when your wedding night comes, it will be strange and painful. But trust your husband. He will show you what to do, and your body will adhere to his actions instinctively. And do not be afraid of the event. Believe me, it is not an ugly sinful act as puritans say. The act of carnal embrace gave me all five of you. How can there be anything evil in it? No, it is the best thing in the world."

"Oh, Mama!"

Jane and I embraced her, and she laughed.

"Oh, so I did that well? Yes, I am glad that I did."

Soon after she finished her advice, she left the room.

"Do you really think that the discord in their marriage sprang from one argument that went on for too long?" Jane asked me.

"She believes so. Sadly, we cannot ask Father if that was what really sparked the series of events where they both lost respect for each other."

"I do not believe that they lost mutual respect entirely."

"Jane, I cannot agree with you. But what we do know is that, somewhere along the string of events that mark their lives together, something did go entirely wrong."

"That is true, at least. Elizabeth, we must promise ourselves to listen to her advice. For it was wise and sound. I do believe that she has learned a lot from today, and she really does wish to help us in the right sort of way. In marriage, there will always be vexation and grief. But we must always try and rise above those moments and overcome them."

"It shall be easier than most marriages," I said, "for Darcy and Bingley are the right sort of men to marry. They are considerate and loyal. That being said, yes, we must always try to not let any disagreements become perpetual and break the foundations of our married life. We do not want to lose their good opinions or their love."

"It would kill me if Mr. Bingley lost his love for me."

"It will kill your heart, but you would have your children to cherish. Either way, yes, for the first time, our mother's advice was perfect. Imagine though, if she had not had that argument with Father, and they recovered, our lives would have ended differently."

"Yes, it would have."

"The could-have-beens and what should-have-beens of life."

Jane took my hand.

"Tomorrow, we are to be the happiest women in the world. We will not let anything get in the way."

"No, we will not."

She left me alone to try and fall asleep. Yet, when the most important day of your life is after the night you are experiencing, sleep will not find you.

***

The next day, the house was a stir with everyone preparing themselves for the events of the day. Before going to the church, we finally had our final guests: Earl and Lady Fitzwilliam, of Matlock, Colonel Fitzwilliam's family. Their eldest son, Victor, was not present for the event, because he was racing horses in a London sporting event.

"And we are the better for it," Mr. Darcy whispered to me, before I got dressed for our happy day. "Cousin Victor enjoys wine too much and is unreliable."

Earl and Lady Fitzwilliam were both agreeable people, and Lady Fitzwilliam obviously favored her younger son, who appeared to be her image of an ideal. Yet, due to the busy air of the household, we did not have the time to become better acquainted, so it would have to occur after I returned as Mrs. Darcy.

We all went to the church, and when all had been seated, Uncle Gardiner was standing at the church doors, with his arms linked around Jane and me.

"I am sure that your father is looking down on you both and is very proud," he offered.

"Thank you, uncle," I said. "I believe he is."

"And he is happy that you are here in his place," Jane spoke.

"When it was your wedding day," I asked him, "were you also this nervous?"

"I sweated until the reverend said that we were now husband and wife."

We both laughed, then he turned to Jane.

"Goodbye, Miss Jane Bennet." Then he turned to me. "Goodbye, Miss Elizabeth Bennet. You walk down this aisle one way and leave it an entirely different woman."

"We are so proud to have you as family," I said.

"Yes, we are," Jane echoed.

The music swelled, the doors opened, and everyone turned to see Jane and me as our grooms stood on either side of the reverend. We walked down the aisle and I looked around, seeing all our family.

Everyone was smiling, except for Mama, who was crying.

"I didn't intend to cry," Mama whispered to Aunt Gardiner. "I didn't intend to cry."

We reached the end of the aisle and we stood beside our soulmates. Looking at Mr. Darcy, our eyes twinkled as we looked at each other, and we had to tear our eyes away and look at the reverend as he read us the marital rites.

A short distance away, stood Colonel Fitzwilliam, who served as best man for them both. He was their best man! This placed him in the awkward position of having to hand the ring to the man who was marrying the woman that he loved. Dear lord! How was he surviving?

The reverend continued to narrate the proper words for the ceremony, and then Colonel Fitzwilliam had to produce the rings. Easily, he handed Darcy his, but his hand was shaky as he handed Bingley his. Taking one last fleeting look at Jane, Colonel Fitzwilliam maintained his composure and looked away from her, shedding any past feelings.

The reverend continued, eventually asking us if we took each other to be our lawfully wedded husband and wife. Mr. Bingley, Mr. Darcy, Jane, and I all gave our affirmation. Next, he asked the witnesses if any of them objected, impeding to our marriage being fulfilled. My heart quickly fell and rose again when no one spoke up.

"Then I now pronounce you husband and wife," he said to Darcy and me, then he turned to Bingley and Jane, "and husband and wife. Go forth into the world as two people made into one."

Everyone cheered, we laughed as we turned around and faced them all. Then we walked out of the church, where rice was thrown over us, and arches of wreathes were placed over our heads as we went back to the carriages and headed back to Pemberley. Once Mr. Darcy got me back into the carriage, I leaned forward, and we kissed eagerly.

"I am yours now," I said.

"And I am yours," he responded.

"Heaven help us."

He laughed.

We returned to Pemberley, where Mrs. Reynolds arranged a beautiful meal for us. Congratulations flowed in, and subsequently led to stories being told.

Mama told us the story of her wedding day.

Aunt and Uncle Gardiner told us theirs.

Earl and Lady Fitzwilliam also indulged us.

And as Mrs. Reynolds was arranging for a new batch of refreshments to be brought in, I took the opportunity.

"Mrs. Reynolds, what was your wedding day like?"

She blinked, surprised that I was addressing her.

"Me?" she asked.

"Yes."

"Oh, it was the busiest day of my life! Everything went wrong. My dress ripped as I walked down the aisle."

We all gaped at her.

"Oh dear," Lady Fitzwilliam exclaimed, "however did you manage?"

"Oh, that didn't stop me. I was determined to have Mr. Reynolds for a husband, so I walked down the aisle and snatched him up."

We all laughed.

As the day progressed, Sir Aleck detached himself from the group and approached Darcy and me.

"Mr. Darcy," Sir Aleck requested, "I am a scallywag for separating you from your fair bride, but I must ask, can I have a private word with you?"

Darcy gave me a look and nodded.

"Very well."

Both men left and I sat alone for a second, taking some peace from all the talking I had done for the day. Of course, my moment of peace could not last.

"Mrs. Darcy," Elena said, "that is what I must call you now."

"Now we are fully family," I said as she sat down beside me. "Can you stomach me?"

"I will do my best," she teased. "Elizabeth, I didn't tell you this sooner, because it was an important time for you, but I thought it best to tell you now."

"Tell me what?"

"My mother has written back to me. She apologizes for she and my father's overreaction. She seeks reconciliation."

"But how do you feel about that? It is always good to forgive, but would it be easy for you to forget?"

"That is the problem. I cannot. It is difficult. Also, they rejected me when I made a mistake and only accepted me again once it was convenient for them. But what happens when I make another mistake?"

"You are afraid that they can't be trusted."

"Yes. And…in truth, I don't wish to go back home. It was a dead house, and I was always dying alongside it."

"Then don't. I will talk to Darcy, and you will stay with us as long as you like, until you are ready to go back home."

"Oh, Lizzy!" She embraced me.

Soon, Sir Aleck and Darcy returned, and they approached us.

"Miss Elena," Sir Aleck asked, "I was wondering if you were willing to look at a fair prospect by that window. The grounds look so beautiful from that angle."

It was a window that was on the furthest side of the room, away from the rest of us.

"Yes," she agreed, "I would love to see it."

Together, they walked to the other side of the room, and Darcy sat by me once more.

"I made a decision while you were gone," I informed him, "but I only did it because I knew that you would have agreed and would have wanted to do it yourself."

"What did you do, you wicked creature?"

"Calm yourself, succubus, I merely told Elena that she can stay with us as long as she needs. She is not ready to go home."

"Then she might be happy with what is about to happen."

"And what is that?"

"She is about to receive an offer of marriage."

I gasped. "What?"

"Yes. Sir Aleck had just asked for my permission to propose to Elena. Since her father is not here, he figured that I substituted for him in his place. I gave him my consent, provided that he respects whatever answer that Elena gives, and writes to her parents afterwards."

I was still a little overwhelmed.

"Give me a moment to collect myself from the shock."

"Take your minute."

I breathed out and in, and then began to laugh.

"And there is the reaction that I was waiting for," he remarked.

"I cannot believe it. Often, love and marriage do not always coincide, with many marriages made out of financial arrangements. But for us, there is not only love at a marriage, but a proposal as well? Now this will be a wonderful story to tell our children."

"You do not feel as if it belittles our beautiful day."

"Not at all. For, if she does accept him, we can boast of being the couple who brought about another marriage. And if she refuses… well, no one needs to know about that, now do they?"

"No, they do not."

Suddenly, we all heard a cry from the other side of the room as Elena was smiling, showing her appreciation.

"And that is the side of the coin that the shilling fell," I observed. "Husband, we have a new couple on our hands."

"Whatever is the matter over there?" Earl Fitzwilliam asked.

"There is no problem, sir," Elena responded, giddily, "I can assure you that it is quite the reverse."

"I have some very good news," Sir Aleck said, taking Elena's hand and walking to the group, "but I do not know if it is correct for me to announce it on another person's special day."

"We do not mind," Darcy affirmed, "I can assure you."

"That is very good of you, cousins," Elena voiced, her cheeks flushed from excitement.

"Everyone," Sir Aleck announced, "first I would like to admit that I am the worst sort of man, and selfish sort of creature who would dare to impede on another person's happiness by announcing his own. I will only speak if you all still promise to remember that this is the wedding day of two of the greatest couples in the world, and this is how this day will be remembered, and not for us."

"I'll speak for them all," I said, "we agree."

"Thank you. Now I can continue by saying that there is a woman here, whose beauty, bounty, and benevolence captivated my heart when I first met her, to the point where I could not go another day without asking her to be my wife. Therefore, that will explain to you the path that led to me losing all self-control and proposing to Miss Elena Darcy just now."

Everyone perked up and began to murmur things, being incomprehensible all the while.

"Well," Lady Fitzwilliam said, "you look happy, Miss Darcy, but we must hear the words."

"I accepted," Elena declared. "I accepted him wholeheartedly!"

Everyone stood up and rushed to the new happy couple. Kitty remained in the back of the enthusiastic crowd.

"Yes," Elena said to them all, "we have decided that we will be the third happiest couple in the world."

"She made that decision alone," Sir Aleck said, "but I am happy that she did."

Moving from Darcy's side, I went to Kitty, who still remained in the background, and I linked arms with her.

"I am happy for her," Kitty said, soberly.

"I know that you are. Kitty, I promise, you will recover and be as joyful again as you once were."

"I know that I will be. I just must remember to keep breathing. If I can do that, then I can remember to place one foot in front of the other. And if I do that, then I know that all will work out well, in the end. However, for the moment, in a few minutes, will you let me excuse myself, on the grounds that I have a headache?"

"Yes, you may, of course."

"I worry that if I stay here, scenes might arise that will be unpleasant for anyone to witness."

"I understand."

We all toasted to the new couple's happiness and hoped to see them speedily married.

After a few minutes, I escorted Kitty out of the room, but she grabbed my hand and pulled me to the music room. Swiftly, she sat down on a sofa and covered her face as she began to weep. I wrapped my arms around her and let her cry into my neck.

"Elizabeth, I feel as if I am dying," she whispered. "I feel as if I am dying."

"I know, and I wish that I could do something. I am sorry that nothing I say will change anything."

"I thought that I was recovering. Truly, I did. I tolerated their flirtations, and their company. Indeed, I really thought that my heart was learning to forget him and fly above this pain. But something changed in this last minute. It felt as if it had been when I first saw them in love. I fell back into that same moment of despair. What happened?"

"The engagement. The shock of it took you by surprise and cemented the history that began to cause you dread. They are engaged now, which is more serious than a mere flirtation. You had no choice but to be affected and your spirit disturbed. But remember, this does not change anything. It does not mean that you are any less worthy than Elena to be the object of a good man's affections. Rather, I think you have the strength to rise above that situation. You are making a life for yourself. If you married Sir Aleck, a man who is always called on to be at parties and dinners, then would you have time to write?"

"Oh, that is very true."

"Sir Aleck is a great man... but he was not a great man for you. And he was not good enough for you either."

"Thank you, Elizabeth. I still am heartbroken, but I do feel better."

"I am happy that I could do that much. In times like these, all the words in the world usually do not make anything better. Go to your room, and I will send Margaret to tend to you. No one will take your absence amiss."

She wiped her face, then went upstairs to her room.

Going back to the party, I offered them her excuses, and everyone wished her well, but returned to speaking of the present weddings and future wedding of Sir Aleck and Elena.

Except that Darcy had a heartbroken cousin sitting with us, who was probably falling apart inside, and my sister was falling apart in her room, it was a perfect day for a wedding. And it remained so, for the people who were hurt knew that we were still in their hearts.

CHAPTER 17

NO LONGER ELIZABETH BENNET

hen the party dissolved, between the Fitzwilliams leaving for Matlock, and everyone else retiring early, Mrs. Reynolds escorted me to my new bedroom—which was next to Mr. Darcy's.

When I entered, it, I gazed at its beauty.

"This is where I am to be Mrs. Darcy?" I took a spin around the room. "Mrs. Reynolds, it is all so beautiful."

"Yes, it is. Oh, my dear, you made such a beautiful bride."

"I did?"

"Your sister may be hailed as the beauty of your family, but I never believed it. I always thought you and Kitty were equally as lovely, just in a different sort of way. But when you walked down that aisle, on your uncle's arm, I saw nothing more lovely. Be good to the master, my dear, be very good to him. He thrives off the loyalty of the people that he loves."

"I can assure you," I promised, "I will spend my life always trying to live up to his good opinion of me. And if I fail, then I'll only start trying again. Thank you for always looking after him, Mrs. Reynolds. You helped raise a good man."

"Oh," she sighed, overcome. At last, she went to the door, and then turned back to me. "Sleep well, Mrs. Darcy."

Closing the door behind her, I sat down, wondering if my servant was going to begin helping me.

And then there was a knock on the door that joined mine with Darcy's bedroom.

My heart began to pace, and I felt the nervousness that Mama often complained of.

But I was not about to let the fears of no longer being a maid keep me from making this an uncomfortable experience. If I was apprehensive and showed any signs of disgust, then Darcy's memory of our wedding night would be a bad one.

I wanted to start making him proud of me.

Therefore, I went to the door and knocked back.

He knocked again, using a different rhythm.

I returned the compliment.

"Elizabeth, are you teasing me?" he asked, through the door.

"Yes. Can't you tell?"

"Can I open the door?"

"Before you do, I want to tell you something."

"Very well."

"Propriety has commanded me to not be as experienced as you. I come to you a maid, as is required. Mr. Darcy, you are my first in everything. My first kiss, my first major love, and the first man—and hopefully last—for me to come to in this sort of way. This offers one attribute: purity. But my condition also offers many problems: lack of experience for another. I had no notion of how to please you, or to make you happy. This will be frightening for me, and terribly uncomfortable—perhaps. But no matter how it is, please remember that it is not how it shall always be. I will learn how to please you over time. I will gather more comfort with this act. But right now, I am a little scared."

"Elizabeth," he responded through the door, "I am prepared, but I thank you for telling me all this. I know that you will make me proud, and I know, due to the burden the world places on you women, you greet this action with fear and trepidation. Our past moments of intimacy still have not fully prepared you for what is about to happen. One thing that I must know. Were you ever taught to fear this action? Or to find it disgusting?"

"Yes," I said, "I've heard older women speak of it as such, sometimes."

"Well, I want you to disregard all of that. There is nothing erroneous or repulsive about this activity. This is one of the most beautiful acts between two people. There is nothing wrong about our desire for each other. Therefore, do not shy away from me, because there is nothing to fear. And do not fear the joys that you will feel from it. Parts of it will be painful, at first. But over time, it will give way to a wonderful moment between us. And soon, you will wish to do it more, and more, and more. And that will make me happy, because I am a very passionate man in that way. Also, if you are worrying that you will not know what to do, often that is the case when it is a person's first time. However, trust your instincts. It is just as it was with our intimacy before. All we must do is start with a kiss, and then all will come afterwards, very naturally and very organically. Do you trust me, Elizabeth?"

"Of course, you fool," I answered, relieved.

"Then I am opening the door now."

"Yes."

Slowly, the knob turned, and the door opened, for us to stand there, facing each other.

"My servant is not coming to help me undress, is she?" I asked.

"I told her not to."

"You always manage to do the right thing. How is that?"

"No idea."

He closed the space between us and kissed me passionately.

"My apologies," he rushed out between kisses, "but I am a little overeager, hence why I cannot do this slowly."

"Slow doesn't always signify being romantic."

"Precisely! Not in this case!"

"Help me get my gown off."

"Damned yes."

He picked me up and carried me over to his bed. When he did so, he turned me around and began to undo my hair. After all the pins were out, I felt his hands undo the fastenings on the back of my dress. Afterwards, it fell on the floor like a pool around my feet.

"Why do women have to wear stays?" he asked as he began to untie the ribbons on it.

"The same reason that men wear neckties," I responded as he

stopped kissing me, "because sometimes we humans make little to no sense at all!"

"I love you."

"I love you as well."

He finally removed my stays and then he quickly raised up my shift and pulled it over my head.

At this point, all that I had on were my stockings that were held up by garters.

Suddenly, Darcy slowed down and he placed his hands on my hips.

"The beauty of your breasts are augmented by the moon's light," he whispered. "And I have never seen anything so beautiful in my life."

He removed his shoes then kissed my neck and ran his hands along my stomach, and then raised them to my breasts, suddenly, he cupped his hands around them and began to massage my nipples between his fingers.

I gasped, amazed by the touch of him.

"This feels beautiful," I exclaimed, my heart beginning to race. "This feels positively beautiful. I missed this terribly."

"There, you see? There is never anything to fear. This is what we are all meant to do. There is no shame in it."

"Yes, no shame at all. I love it!"

"Good," he said, then he lowered his right hand and gently placed it between my legs and touched that place that had never been touched before. He moved his finger over a spot that made me tingle all over, and I moaned aloud, letting him know the pleasure I was feeling. Unable to stop myself, I covered my mouth with my hand.

"Do not worry," he assured me, removing my hand from my mouth. "There is no one on this side of the house, but us. No one will hear you. You may cry out if you wish."

Further and further, he touched my secret spot, and I grew very wet. The wetness began to dampen the insides of my thighs, but I had no time to discover what that was. Nor did I care. It all just felt —right. And beautiful. And quite sensational!

Then Darcy increased his speed, driving his fingers faster and faster within me as his other hand ran their fingers all over my breasts and continued to rock me in the raptures of his embrace.

"Elizabeth?"

"Yes?" I could barely speak for something within me needed release very badly.

"It's time. I've tried to prepare you for this to the best of my ability. Just remember that I am here, and you will grow to love it."

I laid on the bed and he positioned himself on top of me. I was breathless with anticipation as we kissed as he ran his hands over my hair, and then I felt him unfasten his trousers. When finished, he placed himself inside of me and began to push.

I gasped. The pain of it! The searing pain as I felt myself no longer being a maid, but now a wife.

Why were we women made to endure this pain? What did we do to deserve it?

At first, I began to weep a little, but Darcy only pressed his face against mine, though still driving himself further within me.

"Remember that I am here," he assured me. "I am with you."

"You are with me," I whispered.

"Elizabeth, I am with you."

"You are with me." I pressed my lips against his cheek.

"And I am never leaving."

"You are never leaving."

"And you are my wife."

"You are my husband and—it has stopped hurting."

"How does it feel now?"

"Still hurts a little, but I am beginning to like it."

"You are?"

"Yes. I feel you…we are one."

"Yes, we are. My love, I must go faster. You feel beautiful."

"I am ready," I said, holding him tighter, as if I needed him to anchor my anxieties.

"My brave Lizzy."

Suddenly, he began to drive himself faster and faster within me. The more he did so, the more open that I became, and the wetter I made the sheets around us.

"Is this natural?" I asked, breathless. "My wetness?"

"Yes. You are prepared," he rushed out, his voice hoarse.

Suddenly the anticipation became reality. My body flooded with sensations and feelings like I had never known existed. It reached such a peak of pleasure that I felt I might faint from the glory of it. Unable to control myself, I arched my back and moaned. And kept moaning.

He was right. I was no longer afraid, nor was I in any pain at all.

I was happy. Deliriously so.

We were one.

Suddenly, his body spasmed, and with one final thrust, he was complete.

"I am finished," he whispered, then he collapsed on top of me.

"How long did you wish to do that to me?" I asked as I stroked his hair, so very, very, content.

"You have no idea."

CHAPTER 18

A NEW WORLD

*Y*es, I awoke to a new world!

When I opened my eyes, the first thing that I saw was Mr. Darcy sleeping. After we had been intimate, I did not return to my room, but remained in his. Falling asleep next to him was the most comforting thing in the world.

Therefore, I just rested, and allowed myself to stay with him, until he woke.

He opened his eyes. "Oh, good, you are awake."

"You were awake for how long?" I asked.

"About an hour. I just liked watching you sleep."

"I was about to engage myself in that same activity."

His face was beginning to have stubble on it, so I ran my fingers over it.

"So, a man wakes up to find himself hairier."

"Unless he has the good fortune to not grow it at all."

"I'm curious," I said, "when did you first begin to grow facial hair?"

"When I was fifteen. I once knew a boy who started growing his when he was ten."

"Really?"

"Yes. The poor lad. He felt very insecure over that. And he had a reason to. He was bullied over it. But I didn't have time to offer him much solace, because I was too busy learning to not stutter."

"You once had a stammer?"

"Only when I spoke in public. Which, naturally, led to me suffering a little bit of public ridicule. I had to take special lessons to learn how to rid myself of my stammer."

"I never would have known that you went through that," I said. "Darcy, I am sorry."

"Thank you." Suddenly, he remembered himself. "Good lord, here I am, with my brand new wife, and I am talking about my past tragedies."

"That's the beauty of being married," I said, splaying my hand over his chest, "is that you can tell me these things, and it is best that it comes naturally. I can tell you all the ways that I was bullied when I was a child."

"You?"

"I've got a secret," I said, "everyone has been bullied at one time or another. I *didn't* learn to defend myself from it being my nature. I learned how to defend myself to make up for all the times that I didn't before. When I was too young and insecure to rise against those who cast aspersions at me. But never mind now. Because we have no choice but to wake up and greet the world— and the relatives that occupy it. And we must make sure all the preparations for the ball are complete for tonight."

"Why did we agree to a ball the day after our wedding?"

"I know not. For, now that I have time to reflect on it, this was a foolish thing to do. Can we trust in Mrs. Reynolds and Georgiana to do everything, and all we have to do is just come in at the end and say, 'very good, we approve of everything'?"

"I like that scheme. Mrs. Reynolds has planned a few balls before. I know that I can trust her."

"Good," I said, "in the meantime, do you know that activity that we did last night?"

"How could I forget?"

"How could you not indeed? Well, what I must ask is... can we do it again?"

He smiled and rolled on top of me.

"With great enthusiasm."

After a couple of hours, we did meet with our family again, and briefly sat down with them for tea, before all the ladies had to retire to get prepared for the ball. Darcy and I quickly approved of everything that Mrs. Reynolds and Georgiana had achieved and began to prepare ourselves.

A few hours later, carriages were seen driving down the road and the stablemen arranged where they would be placed as the guests stepped out of them.

Darcy, Georgiana, and I stood there to greet them all as they entered, and the rest of our family members stood around the room, preparing to meet them as well.

All the major families had come from all the other great houses in the area for this ball and it was a unique experience. For these were my new neighbors.

"At last," a Mr. Bell said as he bowed to me, "Pemberley gives a ball and gives the rest of us something to talk about for a change. And you are the new Mrs. Darcy."

"I am, sir," I said with a smile, "and you will have to learn to stomach me."

"That can be easy to do, for you have a sense of humor. That is good. Mr. Darcy has always needed a woman who can make him smile."

The Pemberley ball had proven to be enjoyable and laborious. There was something tedious about hosting something, and yet, it presented a spark of life.

Sir Aleck was the one to offer a hearty song of congratulations to Mr. Darcy, Mr. Bingley, Jane, and me. No one doubted his right to do so, because Sir Aleck appeared to be the most popular man in the British aristocracy. Even when it wasn't his ball, it still might as well have been. Mr. Bingley seconded this kindness by also announcing his congratulations on Sir Aleck's being engaged to Miss Elena Darcy. When realizing that they were celebrating a double wedding and recent engagement, the guests became more animated, and all wanted to know the stories about how our happy ending was brought about.

When it came to the dancing, we married couples led it, but Sir Aleck and Elena came next.

Lydia, Mary, and Kitty were never in want of partners at all. Being the single ones in our family, the young men from the other families found them to be exotic. Mama had been insistent that Mary have as fine a gown as the rest of us sisters, as well as have her hair done up better, for the sake of not shaming Pemberley. As a result, Mary looked quite lovely as well, indicating that perhaps she was never actually plain.

The only thing to worry over from all this was Kitty and the Colonel. However, my worries were not necessary at all. Out of the youngest Bennet sisters, Kitty was the one that Colonel Fitzwilliam was the most comfortable with, therefore they easily fell into each other's company and danced together for the first two dances.

"He doesn't know it," Kitty whispered to me, "but we are kindred spirits, who each need a distraction for the pain that the evening inflicts on us. He helps me endure this all, and I believe that I offer the same. Now don't tell anyone but continue dancing with your new husband."

She went off to the Colonel's side as they sat down with each other…until Mr. Bell's son came and asked Kitty to dance the next set with him. Naturally, Kitty had to say yes, and with her light and easy manner, she excused herself from the Colonel to dance again. Unless I was mistaken, he looked a little downhearted when she left him. Kitty was right; she was his shield.

The ball was a great success, but truly I was happy when it was over. I was rendered even more content when I had no need to begin overseeing the after-ball cleaning. Mrs. Reynolds assured us that servants had spent the previous day resting, so that they would be awake that night to clean everything.

"Mrs. Reynolds," I said, "you are a hero."

"Thank you, dear."

All of us were eager to go to bed and completely retreat from the world.

"Everyone has the right to eat their breakfast in their rooms tomorrow," Darcy ordered. "In fact, I order you all to ring for breakfast to be brought to you."

No one disagreed with him.

Once more, Darcy and I went to his bedroom and became husband and wife under the cover of moonlight.

Though we were exhausted, we had the energy to do that. Twice.

After we finished our intimacy for the second time, Darcy's body was on top of me while I stroked his hair. As I did so, he occasionally ran his hands down my breasts, and would take my nipples in between his teeth and suck on them.

"Are you looking for milk?" I asked, in between gasps.

"With any luck, soon I may," he intoned, as he ran his hands back in between my thighs and drove his fingers deep within me once more.

"Can you do me a favor?'

"Yes?"

"Call me Mrs. Darcy."

"Really?"

"Yes, for that is my name, and I am beginning to enjoy it."

He placed his lips on mine.

"Mrs. Darcy."

The joys and agonies of a wedding being over is that you have peace, but also you have to offer your share of farewells.

Mama, Mary, Lydia, Jane, and Mr. Bingley now were leaving for Hertfordshire.

Colonel Fitzwilliam, Kitty, Aunt and Uncle Gardiner were leaving for London.

And Earl and Lady Fitzwilliam also had to depart for Matlock, informing us that they expected us to visit them and stay there for a week. It was evident that soon after becoming Mrs. Darcy, I would have to soon leave Pemberley to visit another side of the family that I wished to gain their respect.

Georgiana, Sir Aleck, and Elena remained with us, which was a nice comfort. This was good, because Darcy expressly ordered Sir Aleck that they couldn't marry until he met her parents and had a longer engagement to get to know each other better.

"You have to understand my logic," he said to me in our bed one night, after we had made love. "Many marriages are entered into so very quickly and it is for the ruin of all. He loves her now, but she might still be exotic to him. He has to like her even after she is no longer that."

"Does it sound like I'm arguing with you?" I asked, amused. "For that is not so. I actually agree with you."

"Oh! How nice."

A week later, we all did go to Matlock and stayed there for a week. Earl and Lady Fitzwilliam proved to be simple people to please, and they did a great deal of talking. I was happy for it, because the more stories that they told, the more I learned about them.

"But what of your eldest son?" I asked Lady Fitzwilliam as she was showing Elena, Georgiana, and I around their portrait gallery. "What of him?"

"Oh, there is a portrait of him," she said, "let me show you our family portrait over here."

She showed it to us, and it was a large and impressive painting.

"That there is my eldest son, Victor," she said, gesturing to the only man we didn't recognize.

"He appears to be a distinguished man," Elena observed.

"Richard is more so. I wish for you all to believe that I love my sons both, very much. However, I believe that Richard was the one born with all the grace, while his brother was born into the wealth of being firstborn. I wish that I could split up my family's fortune and give it to them equally, but perhaps my dear Richard is better off having a profession. By having to earn his living, it has built his character."

"Colonel Fitzwilliam does possess the noble ease of a man who has learned much in life by experience," I noted, "though I have not met your other son, I can say that you raised a fine boy in the Colonel. But what of Mr. Victor? Will we ever meet him?"

"I wish that he would exert himself, but he is too often dashing here and there. He also is racing horses too often. I admire that he has a hobby to occupy his time, but I wish it were a less dangerous one. Also, he has other indulgences that I do not agree with. We ask for him to come home for various reasons, but he only does such at the times that most surprise us. Never take offense to his lack of attention. It is just his way."

Once more, we looked at Victor and I wondered if I would ever have the displeasure of meeting him. There was a mystery about him. Though, I secretly was happy that he did not come to our wedding. His mother minced words, but I recalled what Colonel Fitzwilliam told me about Victor. His brother was a drunk.

On the last day of our stay, I was in bed with Darcy as we lay in each other's embrace.

"It is not fair that Richard was given nothing, while Victor was given everything, is it?"

"No, it's not," he responded.

"I always understood the instinct to give everything to the eldest, because if it were so, then there is no chance of the siblings quarrelling with each other over their inheritance. Britain has seen what happens when the monarchy did not have a peaceful transition in the past."

"Yes, we've learned from history. No practice will ever be perfect, sadly, and this proves it. It is unfair for the eldest to be rich while the younger is so poor, but at least it helps bring order from out of chaos."

"Also, I forgot to tell you something," I said.

"What?"

"Before I left, I got a letter from mother. She told me that our American cousin, Wyatt Wilson, has had a delay in coming. Apparently, he's a businessman, who owns cotton factories. One of them had caught fire."

"Fire? In a cotton factory? That would be disastrous."

"It was. Half of the factory was destroyed, and fortunately, all his workers were able to get out in time, so there are no casualties. However, this has delayed his visit and he wouldn't come to

Longbourn for another three months, to see to the renovations to his factory."

"Your cousin makes cotton."

"Yes, the cloth that not many people wish to wear. Then again, the same was perhaps once said of linen and muslin. And now everyone wears it."

"I do believe that there is a chance that cotton will one day become prominent. Linen is superior for a woman to wear, but it wrinkles quite easily. Cotton is easier to manage, if only it were less expensive."

"I am happy for this," I gathered, "because if our cousin has factories in America, then he will never want to move to Hertfordshire. Our house will be something he can boast of owning, but he would never want to live there."

"Hopefully so."

"We'll see where fate takes us. In the meantime, now we won't have to go to Longbourn sooner than we hoped."

"I do not mean to sound indelicate, for I do respect Hertfordshire, but I admit that I am happy that we get to stay at Pemberley for a longer time, uninterrupted."

"Except for one thing."

"What?"

"We have to go to London for when Kitty's book premieres."

"Oh, yes. I wonder how that is going for her…"

CHAPTER 19

AFTER ENDURING SO MUCH DIFFICULTY

*W*hen Kitty and the Gardiners arrived in London, escorted by Colonel Fitzwilliam, who rode on horseback alongside their carriage, the animation and fears of a dream coming true filled her and brought a glow to your cheek.

It had been arranged that she would visit Allen & Unwin Publishing House in two days.

"And you promise to come with me and be my comrade through this?" Kitty said to the Colonel as he was about to bid them farewell once they arrived in Gracechurch Street.

"I promise, I will come back to Gracechurch that day and escort you to the publishing house."

"Good." Kitty smiled, reaching out to him, and offering her hand. He took it and an oath rested between them. "In such circumstances, a person needs a friend by them. I may write it alone, but when it comes to walking into battle, strength in numbers is always best."

"You make yourself sound like a soldier, you wild creature," Colonel Fitzwilliam jested.

"Perhaps that will be my next story," she said, "of a woman pretending to be a man who enlists in the army. There have been rumors that it has actually happened in real life."

"I know that it has happened."

"You do?"

"There were rumors about it on the American side during the Revolutionary War. And also, on the British side. Those rumors turned out to be true. You have another idea on your hands now, Miss Bennet. May you always have them."

He rode off, to his headquarters.

"Well," Aunt Gardiner said to Kitty as the servants emerged and began to bring the luggage in. "You and the Colonel are very friendly."

"Because misery loves company," Kitty said. "We are two heartbroken people who need to escape the objects of our affection. We do it by offering each other innocent company."

"Are you sure that he knows that it is innocent?"

Kitty gave Aunt Gardiner a quizzical look.

"Aunt," Kitty corrected, "thank you so much for thinking that I deserved a man's love. That is very sweet of you. But the Colonel has no more romantic feelings towards me than he would a tinker."

"That is good, and I hope that it is the same with you. The Colonel is a delightful man. But men like that must marry for wealth, and I do not want to see you hurt."

"I am already hurt, but it is not the Colonel who makes me feel such. In the meantime," Kitty said as the Gardiner children rushed down the stairs, "I have some children that I have to make comfortable around me again."

Kitty walked up to the children, genuflected, and opened up her arms.

"Your cousin Kitty is returned," she said, "and she is not too old for you all to run into her arms and tackle her onto the floor."

They all raced to her and folded their arms around her.

"I come with stories today," she continued, "and by the end of the week, I just might come with toys."

In two days, Kitty had woken up, got dressed very respectfully and sat by the window, waiting for the Colonel. Duly, he came, and Kitty laughed as she ran out of the house to see him.

"Happy to see me?" Colonel Fitzwilliam asked as he dismounted his horse and tied it up, next to the steps.

"Happy to have my fellow knight riding with me into battle," she said. "Aunt Gardiner has made us some breakfast before we go."

"Good, I am starving."

He entered and my aunt and uncle greeted him cheerfully and the children marveled at his redcoat.

Uncle had to leave for work as Kitty and the Colonel used the chaise to go to Allen & Unwin.

"Nervous?" he asked, along the way.

"Petrified," Kitty admitted. "Forgive me if I talk about anything else but the meeting."

"Really?"

"It might help me relax. How have you been since the forty-eight hours that I have seen you?"

"In the little time since we saw each other, so much has happened."

"Really?"

"No, I am merely joking to appear interesting."

Kitty laughed.

"That is the wonderful thing about being born witty," Kitty said, "it helps suffice for when life gets boring. Elizabeth and Lydia were always the amusing ones."

"You don't regard yourself as such?"

"I don't know what I regard myself as, because my character has been changing so much of late, that I wonder where my identity lands."

"You noticed when your character was changing?"

"Yes," Kitty said, "and there is the funny thing about it. I noticed it without influencing it. You know how you sometimes wake up and say to yourself, 'Today, I will try and be more like this'?"

"Yes, I do."

"Well, that's not what I did. I felt my character shifting from one aspect to the next without consequence or consideration. But whenever I was in a new environment, I felt my character meld around the setting."

"That shows a desire to understand that there are certain ways to behave in society and that you are developing yourself. It's good to be aware that you are changing, while it's also good to not feel as if you must have a defined character as of yet. Forcing your personality to take on a definitive shape is dangerous for your mind in the long run. By letting yourself shift about so organically, it will lead to you being happy in the end."

"Yes, I do believe that I am willing to adhere to such a rule but am not ready to fully write my character yet. And I like it."

"So do I."

"Thank you. Was that how you arrived at the man you were? By letting your character drift around, from one attitude to the next, until you settled in your proper place?"

"I never thought about it before, until now, but I do believe that I did do that. When I was young, I was very insecure about all the pimples that I had, and fortunately, they left over time."

"And now you have a clear face."

"Was your face always clear?"

"No, I had pimples as well, every now and again. Fortunately, they were not profuse. Mary had it the worst, which I wonder is what led to her wishing to be so accomplished."

"Me having pimples helped me wish to excel at the pianoforte as well, so I can well believe it. What we humans do to compensate for our flaws."

"Then you could argue that it is better to have flaws, because it gives us all something to strive against."

The carriage arrived.

"There, you see?" Kitty remarked, with a raised eyebrow. "I was never given time to get nervous."

They entered Allen & Unwin Publishing House and were met by an incredible surprise. They were met by Mr. Unwin, who not only returned Kitty's manuscript, but had a hard copy of the novel produced for her to quickly peruse before publishing.

"I cannot believe it," Kitty cried, holding the cover of the book and the golden engraved letters. "You did all this so very quickly!"

"Well, we were given the proper amount of encouragement,"

Mr. Unwin said, "for we were given an express order to be quick about it."

"Ordered?" Kitty asked. "I thought I was humble in the letter."

"You were, but you have friends in high places and..." he trailed off when she did not know what he was talking about. "Am I correct in assuming that you are not aware that we received a letter from the right honorable Lady Catherine de Bourgh?"

Kitty blinked and looked at the Colonel, who also indicated his ignorance of the subject.

"No," Kitty said, "I did not. Lady Catherine sent a letter to you all?"

"Yes," he said, removing the letter from his desk. "It was quite the surprise. From what I understand, you are well-acquainted with her."

"Not enough that I thought I deserved any special recognition. I stayed with her for a time, and now we are related through family."

"Yes, Mr. Darcy is her nephew."

"And so is the Colonel."

Mr. Unwin looked at Colonel Fitzwilliam with new reverence.

"Good gracious, are you?"

"Yes, sir. Her brother, the Earl of Matlock, is my father."

Mr. Unwin smiled at Kitty.

"You family has made a fortunate alliance."

Kitty smiled a shy smile. "Something I wish I could take credit for, but it was not my doing."

"Well, you did enough. Lady Catherine sent an express order for me to arrange for your book to be published as soon as proper, and she forwarded one hundred pounds to us, to do it."

Kitty's mouth dropped open.

"She did that for me?!"

"She did."

Kitty looked down at the book, which was beautiful, and the title shined in the light 'Truth & Trivialities'.

"I promise that I will have it read by the end of the week and will let you know if there are any errors."

"Very good. The sooner that it is completed, the sooner that we can publish it. Announcements will be in the papers, informing everyone of its being available here, and we shall have a display for it upon release. We have the contract written up here. Never fear, it is in plain speech, and I can assure you that the royalties that you receive are the proper amount, bar the price of the book printed, and our fee is taken out. It is a standard contract that all authors receive."

"I checked other publishing house fees," Kitty informed him, "so that I would not be ignorant about it and waste your time."

Kitty and the Colonel took the contract and read over it.

"The amount is correct," Kitty informed the Colonel, "but is the wording proper?"

"It is," Colonel Fitzwilliam assured her. "There is no trickery here."

"Good."

They went back to Mr. Unwin and Kitty signed the contract.

On the way home, Kitty and the Colonel were laughing merrily.

"I cannot believe it!" Kitty cried. "I didn't even notice that Lady Catherine cared for me at all."

"And all that time, she cared for the part you were involved in when bringing Anne home. She never said thank you because she had meant to show it in another way."

"And by helping me, she also can say that she apologized for how she treated my sister and Darcy when they were engaged, without saying it. For, by helping me, she has redeemed herself. Oh, that woman! She destroys and then saves us all. How can I repay her, besides sending her a letter? Does she like anything particular that I can afford?"

"Begin with the letter, and I will think of something."

"So, now that I have good news, I wish to celebrate. Will you come with me back to Gracechurch Street? Aunt Gardiner might give us a cup of punch."

"When receiving a cup of punch is the epitome of celebrating, that is very charming," he said, "but alas, I have to go to the army grounds and check on my soldiers' new uniforms. Their older ones were getting too shabby, and I have to make certain that these new ones are up to snuff."

"Oh," Kitty said, "then can I go with you? We never told my aunt when we would return, so I do have time. Can I not go with you?"

"It is just uniforms," he laughed.

"And I am just a writer who needs to know as much as she can about soldiers. Until now, I never saw how uniforms were distributed, and now I get to see it. And I will get to see army grounds. You are used to living that life, but for me, it will be another adventure. Please, Colonel, help me gather a wider acquaintance with the ways of the world, and decrease my ignorance of it. Let us imagine, for a second, that I am allowed to be the luckiest creature in the world, and people actually read my books and the publisher wanted me to write another one. If I am to write, I must know things. If I will promise to be very quiet and not say anything there, will you take me along?"

"Why would I want you to be quiet?" he asked, amused. "Silence is for married couples who can't stand to hear the other one speak. We are now cousins."

"Precisely."

Colonel Fitzwilliam told our driver to take us to the army grounds instead.

"And if anyone gets mad with you for taking me away," Kitty assured him, "I will take all the blame on myself. I am accustomed to that happening to me."

"I am sorry that I was not there to defend you when that happened."

"I wish you were as well, Colonel."

They reached the army grounds and Kitty marveled at all the officers that they passed, as well as the training that she witnessed. Eventually, they reached the warehouse where the uniform distribution was, and Colonel Fitzwilliam did his check-in.

"Is there any way that I can help?" Kitty asked. "Or am I useless?"

"No, since I know that you know how to write." He handed her a list and told her to write down the amount of each size that he checked. When they neared the end of it, Colonel Fitzwilliam looked at her. "I am boring you."

"Not at all," Kitty said. "I was just thinking of when I was back home, in Hertfordshire, when Colonel Forster's regiment was stationed there."

"The age of Wickham."

"I refuse to let his shadow cast a darkness on everything. Before all that controversy, Lydia and I were accomplices. We often travelled to Meryton to see them so often. I do not deny that I was stricken with redcoat fever that has plagued so many women. If a man was in a redcoat, then I raised him up as a prince among men. And then Wickham proved that redcoats did not indicate anything about the man who wore it."

"It is good not to base a man on his uniform rather than his character, but I hope that you had not developed a prejudice towards us recoat-wearing characters."

"You know that I haven't." Kitty tilted him a glance and tapped his shoulder playfully. "You are not bad company at all."

After a while, they finished, and all the uniforms appeared to be in good condition.

"Well, you were of great assistance," he complimented her.

"And I was not bored at all." She looked around the room. "Redcoats without officers to fill them... now that is a sight."

They were interrupted when a man suddenly burst in.

"I am looking for Colonel Fitzwilliam," he said. "I was told he was in this office."

"I am Colonel Fitzwilliam," he said, stepping forward, "whatever is the matter?"

"I am a messenger. I was sent to give you this."

The messenger handed him a letter and Colonel Fitzwilliam sliced it open and began to read it immediately. Kitty quietly watched him as the Colonel's face slowly turned white. He lowered the letter and stood there, frozen.

Seeing his shattered state, Kitty walked up to the messenger and gave him a few pennies for his service. He thanked her and left. When she turned around again, Colonel Fitzwilliam was still standing there, motionless.

Feeling as if she was watching a spooked animal, Kitty didn't know what to do. The silence was deafening. At last, Kitty took a step forward.

"Colonel?" she asked. "Richard?"

"I have to take you home."

"Good god, what is the matter?"

"It's my brother, Victor. He was racing his horses against another set of gentlemen here in London, and he was thrown. He is dead."

Kitty couldn't believe her ears.

"Dead?" she repeated. "There must be some mistake. Perhaps the news was incorrect."

"Let us pray so," he spoke, his tone grave and almost with a hint of hissing rage. "If he is dead, I will never forgive that fool."

Without knowing it, he grabbed Kitty's hand and led her away.

"I have to take you home."

"But you don't have time for that," Kitty said. "You have to go and see him now. I'll go with you."

"Kitty, I do not mean to burden you with my family's affairs."

"But we are family now," she pointed out, "and I was the one who happily accepted your company with my book, therefore, I had best be prepared to be equally as empathetic. Besides, you waste time by taking me home."

Up ahead, she saw the messenger who was about to climb his horse and depart. Rushing forward, she called to him.

"Please wait," she said, then she rushed up to him again and offered him four shillings. "Are you capable of remembering an address and sending a verbal message?"

"Yes. Provided the address is easy."

"It's 504 Gracechurch Street."

"Oh, around the corner of the factory? Mr. Gardiner's home."

"You know my uncle?" she asked, amazed.

"My sister works for him at the factory."

"Small world indeed. That is good. I need you to go there and tell my aunt that I have to go with the Colonel, to give him company due to a loss in his family."

"Very good, Miss," he said, tipping his hat, climbing his horse, and dashing off afterwards. Kitty turned back to the Colonel.

"We have done our duty by them," Kitty said, "now it is time that we care about you."

Happy to have her company, they set out in the chaise again, and Colonel Fitzwilliam ordered to be taken to the racing grounds. When he got there, he inquired and was told that his brother's body was sent to the nearest coroner. When given the address, they were redirected and soon arrived there.

When they entered, they were met by two men.

"You must be his brother?" one of them said.

"I am," Colonel Fitzwilliam said, his eyes on fire, "and you are Mr. Roger Peterson and Mr. Franklin Presley. My brother's friends."

"You know us?"

"Yes, though you perhaps forgot. That would make sense because you were too drunk at the time. Now tell me, is my brother really there?"

"Yes," Mr. Presley confirmed.

Colonel Fitzwilliam moved around them, Kitty curtsied to both of them and then followed him. Briefly they met with the coroner, who took them into the storage room in the mortuary. On the table, there was a body that was covered in cloth.

Kitty was too stunned to get closer, but the Colonel gathered his courage and stepped forward as the coroner removed the cloth enough to show the victim's face.

"Is this your brother, sir?" the coroner asked.

Colonel Fitzwilliam just stared down at the dead man.

"Is it your brother, Victor Fitzwilliam?" the coroner repeated.

"Yes," Colonel Fitzwilliam whispered, finally able to answer, "that is Victor." Placing his hands on the sides of his brother's dead face, he was desperate. "For God sakes, get up, damn you! You're playacting. You always used to playact. Stop playacting!"

"Sir—"

"Why?" Colonel Fitzwilliam hissed. "Why are you dead? You spent too much of your life not listening! Why couldn't you listen? Why could you never do the right thing?"

Finding the courage to act, Kitty went up to the Colonel and wrapped her arms around his shoulders.

"Come away, Richard," she advised, "come away."

He allowed himself to be pulled away from his brother's corpse as the coroner placed the cover back over the body. Giving into his despair, Colonel Fitzwilliam fell into Kitty's embrace as his knees gave way and he collapsed on the floor. Crouching down, Kitty held him.

"We were so close as children," Colonel Fitzwilliam continued to weep, "he was great as a child. We don't know what happened. We don't know what happened."

As Kitty held him, she looked up at Victor's covered up corpse. It was her first-time facing death, and now it all felt so real. Too real.

CHAPTER 20

DIFFICULT TIMES

*D*ressed in black, Darcy, Elena, Sir Aleck, Georgiana, and I were traveling from Pemberley to Matlock. Upon hearing that the funeral service for Victor Fitzwilliam was to take place at the parsonage on the estate, we traveled there.

"Have you ever met Victor?" Elena asked me.

"In the brief time that I have been in the family," I said, "no, I did not. But I am sorry, Darcy and Georgiana."

"I am sorry for our aunt and uncle," Georgiana said. "This will be hard for them."

"We were never close to Victor, I confess," Darcy augmented. "He did not understand temperance at all."

"Far be it from me to speak ill of the dead," Sir Aleck said, "but with each time that I invited him to one of my balls, he ended it needing to be escorted from the party."

"Really?" I asked.

"Yes. For all that we know, he could have grown into a wiser man in the end, but sadly fate had other plans. But when it comes to children, parents do not care about their flaws, because their love runs deeper than that."

When we arrived, Colonel Fitzwilliam and Kitty were outside, waiting for us. Because it was a warm and sunny day, they had been walking along the grounds together. When I saw them out of the window, I wondered at the sight of them together.

Kitty had been the one to write the letter to us about the funeral. From what we understood, she had been there when Colonel Fitzwilliam was told about his brother's death, they went back to Gracechurch Street to tell our aunt and uncle the new loss in his family, and Kitty offered to join the Colonel in returning home, delivering his brother in a coffin. As a result, she was now a guest there.

When we stepped down, we women rushed to her, and she embraced us all.

"Even though it has not been very long since I saw you three," Kitty said, "it feels like it has been ages." Looking at us all, she was overjoyed. "I missed you all. I hope you missed me a little."

"Oh, more than a little," Georgiana said as the men accosted the Colonel and offered their condolences.

"My parents will be happy to see you all," Colonel Fitzwilliam said. "Come in before we leave for the church. They are in need of a little more merriment."

We entered and Earl and Lady Fitzwilliam were glad of our company.

"Oh, thank goodness," Lady Fitzwilliam said, "in such troubling times, it is good to have more family around you."

"I am sorry, Aunt," Georgiana said, embracing her.

"Yes, the word sorry is going about everywhere," Earl Fitzwilliam voiced, bitter. "I am sorry for not ordering him to stay in Matlock, his mother is sorry for not curbing his temptation, we're all sorry for the pain he inflicted, yes, everyone is sorry, but the man himself. I told him not to race horses. Mark it down that I told him! But he is not here to apologize. He will never speak again."

"My dear, please…" Lady Fitzwilliam said, patting his leg.

"Forgive me," he said to all of us.

"There is nothing to forgive," I assured him. "You are a family in distress and have suffered in a way that no parent should. Your feelings are natural and just."

"No parent should have to see their child die," he voiced, heartbroken, "no parent."

"Life has dealt you all a terrible blow," Kitty said. "All we can hope for is that your son has found peace. His worldly cares are over."

"And ours are still very deep. But thank you, dear."

"Miss Kitty has been a great comfort to us," Lady Fitzwilliam said to me.

I looked at my baby sister with pride. "I am sure that she has."

We rode to the church and stood at Victor's grave as he was being lowered down into it. The reverend continued his kind words as the coffin reached the bottom. Georgiana leaned on my shoulder, and I held her as she wept. Lady Fitzwilliam was doing her best not to be hysterical as the Earl held her and tried to remain strong himself.

The last was Colonel Fitzwilliam, who Kitty stood by, holding his arm.

As inconsiderate of me to care about anything else but the heaviness of death, I couldn't help but be curious. Nudging Darcy, I gestured with my head. He also noticed the two of them, but we said nothing.

Looking down at the coffin being lowered into the ground, I lamented that a man would die so young, and for no reason at all. And he was the Earl's heir.

The heir!

Looking up to Mr. Darcy, I whispered.

"Darcy, Colonel Fitzwilliam is now the heir of Matlock."

"Yes. That is the only good thing that has come out of this. He can now leave the army and he is safe from such a life."

"I apologize for being late!" came a thunderous voice from a short distance away.

We all turned, and Lady Catherine de Bourgh was striding toward us.

And she was not alone.

Mr. and Mrs. Anne Orwell were with her as well.

"Lady Catherine!" Kitty cried.

"There was a farmer on the road with cows that wouldn't move," Lady Catherine said, "or we would have been here earlier." The three of them reached us. "There is no earthly way that I would not come when my brother's eldest son is leaving this world for the next."

Earl Fitzwilliam opened his arms to her, and we all saw Lady Catherine embrace him as well. This was such a surprising image, for I did not believe that any of us ever saw her be so warm in her affections before. But now we have.

We greeted Anne and Mr. Orwell kindly as Lady Catherine stood at the foot of the grave.

"I may be late, but I will carry my point," Lady Catherine demanded, "and I will say a few words."

We all lined up and listened.

"Poor Victor," she began, "he was a lovely child, and then he decided to walk down the wrong path. Then he walked down another wrong one. It reached a point where I believed that wrong paths were always something he would choose to peradventure."

We all looked at each other. Even in death, Lady Catherine was herself.

"I always used to find myself lamenting the man you were," she continued, "and wishing that the heir of Matlock was a better creature. But now I wonder if maybe, along the way, I had taken a wrong step myself. Perhaps I should have tried harder to understand you, and help you, rather than scold you and give you no instruction when you came to my house for visits. Perhaps I should have learned to listen to you and see if there was a reason that you always felt the need to escape somewhere else. Perhaps you were looking for an *escape*, and I did not listen. And maybe, just maybe, I am sorry. But it is too late for that now. You have passed over to a better life. And maybe you will find what you were all along and be happy."

"It is not your fault," Lady Fitzwilliam said, "we all perhaps did not listen until it was too late, but my son did make his choices. Either way, that is beautiful, Lady Catherine, and I thank you."

Dirt was placed over the coffin and Victor Fitzwilliam was gone from this world.

We all returned to Matlock to dine. Dressed in black, we were a sober gathering, until Kitty thanked Lady Catherine for her contribution to her book. To much of our surprise, Lady Catherine had been active in quickly getting Kitty's book published.

Lady Catherine took her thanks, and then began to shower her with advice on what to put in her next book. Kitty listened, but it was unknown how much advice she would take.

We all decided to remain with the family for a couple of weeks, to help them through the trying times. What was more to the purpose was that Colonel Fitzwilliam had to now transition from soldier to heir.

"This is the outfit that I will never wear again," Colonel Fitzwilliam said as he packed away his uniform. "And now I will always dress as a gentleman."

"And walk like a gentleman, talk like a gentleman, and speak nonsense like a gentleman," Kitty remarked, in jest.

"And what if I fail at all three of those things?"

"I refuse to allow you to not learn how to speak nonsense. It is one of the best talents of life."

Due to the arrangement of humans to naturally break off into couples, there was a new development on the rise. Kitty and the Colonel often sought each other's company, took solace in each other's words, and found ease even when they had nothing to say.

Darcy saw it.

So did I.

And whatever anxieties I had on that score were not sufficient or valid. I knew that Colonel Fitzwilliam once loved Jane. As I knew that Kitty had been infatuated with Sir Aleck. Their past history indicated two people who perhaps wanted loved in other places, to help them recover from their previous attachments. Such a relationship is not always healthy, because the person attaches themselves to the other for the wrong reasons.

Yet upon closer inspection, that was not what was happening. They both just seemed to like each other…accidentally. Darcy and I were watching them acutely, while also making it appear as if we weren't, and we saw two people falling in love without even noticing that they were.

"I daresay that they are in the middle before even noticing that they had begun," I said to Darcy one day, as we were sitting together, playing backgammon. Kitty and the Colonel were walking together in the gardens, and we saw them from the window. They had taken an old kite from the attic and were now seeing if it flew. When a gust of wind picked up, Colonel Fitzwilliam threw the kite in the sky, and it caught.

We saw Kitty laugh merrily, as Colonel Fitzwilliam closed his hand around hers, to help steady her grip. This act was so organic to them that they didn't even notice or experience any awkwardness from it.

"I wish I could tell them that they are in love with each other," I commented, "but it wouldn't be my place."

"I understand the inclination," he supported, "however, we have no choice. We must let them discover it for themselves. I only hope that it doesn't take them too long. With Victor's death, my aunt and uncle need a happy moment to occupy them. And the knowledge of a wedding, that hopefully will quickly lead to grandchildren, is the precise sort of thing to raise their spirits."

"But I wonder… would your aunt and uncle approve the match? After all, they couldn't control you marrying me, but their son is another matter altogether. They might not think that Kitty is good enough for him, just because of our mother's family. Remember, that almost hindered you choosing me."

"They do not worry over it," he responded, "I can guarantee it."

"How so?"

"Simple. I overheard them talking about it when they didn't know that I was in the opposite room, accidentally hearing every word they said."

"Really?" I arched one eyebrow. "Darcy the eavesdropper. Now that is an interesting title."

"I did not seek it out, but it was thrust upon me."

"Yes, that's the tone."

"Well, my wicked wife, to put it simply, Richard is now the heir and can marry as he chooses. Perhaps, if they were not in such an interesting state, they would prefer if Richard married well. But they don't care about that because they now feel how short life can be. At this rate, all they wish is for Richard to be happy and stay at home. A wife, quickly obtained, will help influence him to stay and quickly begin making a family and a new heir for Matlock."

"Oh, yes, that is true. Richard is now the only chance for Matlock to continue in their line. Therefore, the speed that they wish to achieve this makes Kitty the ideal option, because she's already here, is pretty, educated, makes the Colonel happy, and she's healthy." This observation made me laugh. "They have no choice but to love Kitty immediately. How very fortunate for her. Provided Colonel Fitzwilliam realizes that he loves her, of course. I know that she will easily grow to love him if he gives her a reason."

"You do?"

"Kitty has learned how to be independent, but her heart still beats and is ready for love whenever it chooses to find her."

"Well, I wonder how much longer we all have to—"

He stopped midsentence and gazed out the window.

"What?" I asked, then I followed his gaze.

There, outside, Kitty and Colonel Fitzwilliam were kissing. With their hands still on the kite, their faces were resting against the other and were locked in true affection.

"And apparently we do not have to wait for very long," I said. Mr. Darcy looked at me. "A shilling for your thoughts?"

"Matlock has just found a new Mrs. Fitzwilliam."

"Yes, it has," said a voice behind us.

We turned and it was Lady Fitzwilliam. Having silently entered the room, she had pulled the curtains back so that she could get a further look at the happy couple.

"And about time," she added, "for how long can two people sit in drawing rooms, day in and day out, and not fall in love with so many compatible traits?"

"Can I hope that you like my sister?" I asked. "We may not be in the aristocracy, but when we love, we love truly."

"With all things considered, love is the precise thing that Richard needs. Mr. and Mrs. Darcy, go and get my son and your sister. And tell them that they better have a proper announcement for us. I'll arrange for us all to be in the sitting room, prepared for the news."

She left us to ring the bell for everyone to be summoned.

I turned to him and smiled.

"Well, we have our orders."

"In this matter, it is best to obey."

We went outside and the couple spotted us immediately.

"Did you see us from the window?" Kitty asked.

"Very much so," I replied, "and Richard, your mother has summoned everyone in the sitting room."

"She anticipated me," Colonel Fitzwilliam said, laughing, "my clever mother."

Joy!

That was the mood that everyone felt after the announcement was given. When speaking of their engagement, Kitty and the Colonel couldn't help but chuckle throughout, for they were so happy that it was beyond words.

"Now when you say engagement," Lady Catherine declared, "I'm assuming that you mean that you haven't fixed a date for when you get married?"

"No, we haven't," Kitty answered. "I know that I love him, because it has been coming on so gradually, that I was in the middle before I even began. But I want to give him time to learn if he really does want me for a wife."

"That is arid nonsense if I ever heard it! What more does he need to know? How good you are at sitting home and learning the ways of running a household? Lady Fitzwilliam can teach you all that. Learn that you love each other? Well, you both know that. Understanding each other? You two can boast of being more aware of each other's natures than most people can boast when entering the married state."

"I am of total agreement," Lady Fitzwilliam said. "I advise that you both marry as soon as may be."

"If so, then we could have a double wedding here," Sir Aleck boasted, "for I cannot wait any longer."

"Nor can I," Elena gasped. "Oh, Kitty and Colonel, do so. Please, let us say that we had a double wedding, like your sisters did. If you can bear to share your happy day with us, of course."

"Well," Kitty said, "I know where my heart lies, but if the Colonel does not wish it, then we must not guilt him into rushing into a decision."

We all turned to him.

"Oh, this is not guilt at all," he declared. As we laughed, Kitty went to him and took his hand.

"Do not let anyone influence you, Colonel. Hold to your purpose, and never move just because the world tells you to."

"Tell me that you love me."

"I love you," Kitty declared, her eyes warm and her tone sincere.

Colonel Fitzwilliam turned to the rest of us.

"As soon as Mrs. Bennet and her other daughters come for the ceremony, we will marry."

The room was all in a glorious uproar.

"Do you prefer for us to invite your parents, my dear?" Sir Aleck asked Elena.

"In truth, no. I would much rather marry you and then tell them afterwards. My parents are a dour sort who cannot stand each other. I think it best to get you to marry me now, so that when you meet them, they won't influence you to lose your love for me."

"That is impossible. But are you sure?"

"With every fiber of my being. Besides," she looked at us all, "I prefer the family that I have now."

Elena rushed up to Kitty and grabbed her hands, twirling her around.

"We shall be married on the same day!"

"And irony must have a sense of humor," Kitty laughed, "for it to be so."

"Why is it ironic?"

"I cannot tell you now," Kitty said, "because that would not do at all. But one day I will tell you, when you are older. Georgiana and Elizabeth," she said, opening their hands so that we all could take hands and skip in a circle. "Now we all shall be family even more."

"Who would have thought!" I cried, merrily. "Who would have thought?"

Earl Fitzwilliam ordered for them to marry in no less than a fortnight. So, he sent an express letter to Netherfield Park and Longbourn, expressly desiring them to come by Sunday next, so that they could be present to see his son marry Kitty Bennet. Being a man of action, who desperately wanted his son to start making a new family right away, he made it evident in his letter that the marriage would happen, whether they arrived or not. This naturally forced Mama to quickly make plans with Mr. Bingley, and Matlock saw them all arrive one day before the wedding.

In that time, Lady Fitzwilliam had ordered two new gowns be made for the two brides, and us Bennet sisters and Georgiana were to be their bridesmaids. And now it was Darcy's turn to be the best man.

When my mama arrived with Jane, Mary, Lydia and Mr. Bingley, there was the general noise of family meeting other family, but it was a beautiful sound. Fortunately, the grandness of Matlock was enough to overpower Mama's and Lydia's manners and they were too much in awe of this new great house, to say very much at all. But one thing that was evident was that Lydia was jealous of Kitty.

"I thought that I would be the first between us two to marry," Lydia said. "Kitty, I cannot forgive that you proved me wrong. But give me five minutes, and I'll find a way to turn it into a joke."

"Three daughters married to three of the worthiest and greatest men in England," Mama cried as she embraced Kitty. "Oh, my word! I shall go distracted. Poor Mr. Bennet would have wanted to see this. And I could have finally told him something that I always wanted to say."

"What?" Kitty asked.

"That I was right. I wished to say that, after it was proven, for our entire marriage. Oh well, oh, poor Mr. Bennet. Poor Mr. Bennet." She kissed Kitty. "My dear, I had never expected this to happen when you left Longbourn. I never knew that you would have made the greatest match of them all."

"And to think I just did it out of pure ignorance," Kitty answered, "who could have predicted that the best way to find love was to not look for it? Now there is a maxim that should be set down."

"Well," Mary said, "to add to the good news that we find ourselves, guess what?"

"What?"

"Our American cousin, Wyatt, has written again, telling us that he cannot come, still needing to see to the renovations of his factory. He promises to come one day, expressing his deep regrets that he keeps delaying his visit. In the meantime, he wished to inform us that his visit is merely to see family, and not to claim ownership."

"He wrote that we are to keep Longbourn!" Mama cried. "He made it evident in his letter that it will be in his name, but that we can always live in it, unless one day, there would be no one to occupy it. Oh, he's a very good sort of American."

"Many of them have been known to exist, you know," I said, laughing.

Kitty and I both could have been knocked down with a feather, for we were both astonished.

"So," I extoled, breathless, "we still get to keep Longbourn?"

"Yes," Mr. Bingley confirmed. "Your home will never be taken from you."

"After that fear and anxiety on the matter," Kitty recalled, "and the entire time, it all was leading up to a natural conclusion that was right all along."

"All those years of fearing that Mr. Collins would take Longbourn," Mama said, "and all that time that I complained to your father. Only for us to have been given Longbourn in the end. I wish that I could apologize now to your father, but it cannot be helped."

"He hears you, Mama," Jane assured her. "He hears you."

"Yes, I believe that he does. Oh, Mr. Bennet! If we could have done it all differently... if only we could go back to the beginning... yes. Yes."

"That means that if the rest of my sisters don't get married, then they have Longbourn for a home," I said. "But you know what? If any young man comes for Mary or Lydia, then send them in. For I am quite at my leisure."

The wedding day was quite the frenzy. Everyone was busy at trying to make everything work, but there was confusion. Due to that, the brides and grooms accidentally reached the church at the same time. The men had first arrived in one carriage, and the women in the second.

When they did, Kitty was seized by an idea.

"Let's see who is fastest."

Taking Elena's hand, she began to skip to the church. Quickly seeing what Kitty was about, Elena laughed and skipped as well. Sir Aleck and Colonel Fitzwilliam fell into the merriment of the moment, and they laughed, walking quickly. Both ladies and gentlemen reached the church door at the same time and had to catch their breath.

"What are you all about!" Lady Fitzwilliam called to them.

"We have our entire lives to be normal and give into propriety, Mama," Richard called, breathless. "This is the last moment that we can do something very irregular."

"Now that will be a story that they can tell their children," Mr. Bingley said, then he turned to Darcy. "Darcy, why didn't we do something that unorthodox on our happy day?"

"Bingley, you forget. We spent our entire acquaintance with Elizabeth and Jane being unorthodox. We did everything wrong from the very beginning. Therefore, hopping to the church would have just felt redundant."

"If you did everything wrong," I assured him, taking his hand, "you did it while always wearing a very nice waistcoat."

"You liked my waistcoats."

"Oh, very much. It removed the sting of all our misunderstandings, because I could always say, Mr. Darcy always had a nice waistcoat."

With all of us properly assembled in the church, we Bennet sisters and Georgiana walked down the aisle on the arms of the remaining gentlemen. The grooms waited at the altar, with Darcy to their left and the reverend in between them.

At last, with Earl Fitzwilliam standing in their place of both women's absent fathers, Kitty was on his left and Elena was on his right. Wearing two beautiful gowns of the same color, and having lovely bouquets in their hands, Elena and Kitty walked down the aisle towards their eager grooms. And if I had not known of all the trials and tribulations that had led to such a moment, I would not have believed it. Never would I have believed that Kitty and Colonel Fitzwilliam had never initially been in love. Never would I have believed that Kitty had been jealous of Elena. Never would I have believed that Kitty liked Sir Aleck and Colonel Fitzwilliam had liked Jane. No, but rather, I would have agreed to seeing the perfect arrangement here and insisted that it had been this way all along. All had worked itself out in so proper a manner, in so logical a way, that one could only wonder that it had not been arrived at sooner.

Happy was the day that Mama could give away her second to youngest daughter to the heir of Matlock estate, and to a man who would inherit the title of Earl. For indeed, she now saw the ends of her pursuits in life once more reaching the whole delightful and astonishing conclusion of a happily ever after.

Elena's parents eventually were told of their daughter's marriage to Sir Aleck Granger, the most popular man in the ton and of the legendary estate in Cranford. Of course, what is natural is that they accepted her again, but Elena was aware that they only did so out of selfishness. She met them again, but not often. Most of her time with Sir Aleck was spent either at Cranford, or with us, for she always viewed us as the means for bringing them together.

Mary, Georgiana, and Lydia enjoyed the life of three sisters who had many homes to visit and revisit.

Kitty's first novel did release and was not met with initial success, but with the rise and fall of six months, 'Truth & Trivialities' found a home on the bookshelf of anyone who liked to read. Her publisher demanded 'Romance & Revolution', wishing to capitalize on her success as a writer and Kitty was happy that she finished it already, because she had done right by the Colonel and was immediately with child.

All things end, as they have no choice but to. For anything to begin, an ending must occur. But wherever there is life, there is chance. And wherever there is chance, there is the chance for family. And with family, chance never ends.

With us, chance never ended… because we would always do our best to look for it.

Look for it. That is what I advise you. Just look for it.

The End

Don't miss out on your next favorite book!

Join the Satin Romance mailing list
www.satinromance.com/mail.html